The Dream Journal

MARK FARRAN

Mark Farran

ISBN: 1463738102

ISBN-13: 978-1463738105

DEDICATION

For God, who is worthy of all praise.

CONTENTS

ACKNOWLEDGMENTS

I would first like to thank God for giving me mono and making me physically unable to do anything but sleep, read, and write for six months. I would like to thank my mom for editing the book. I would also like to extend a special thanks to my wife Jamie who encouraged me to write. Without her encouragement I most likely would not have finished the book.

CHAPTER ONE

Like most young teenagers, Matt had an ego complex beginning to grow. He was already taller than most guys in his class and could run faster and jump higher than the majority of them. He began to stand out in the various sports he played. Matt was well built and good looking. His ego was now beginning to effect his relationship with his parents. They could see his pride growing, and as believers they worried about the effect it would have on him.

Matt had grown up in their home as they had attempted to raise him knowing Christ Jesus who was their Lord. The result was that Matt knew a lot about Christ and the Bible. Growing up in Sunday school had left him with lots of Bible knowledge and stories, but none of that ever seemed to impact his life.

At this time Matt was now in his young teen years and still showing minimal signs of any regard for God. He only went to church on Sunday because he didn't want to fight with his parents about it. Matt also rarely went to any youth group events because it wasn't too fun for him. The only time he did go was if he was interested in a girl that was going at the time. He never felt like he learned much there and would much rather spend his time playing basketball at the park.

Matt knew that he had minimal regard for God, but it did not seem to faze him. "I'm not really that bad of a person," he would think to himself, "How bad could I be? I grew up in church, I don't lie, I don't steal anything big, I am not out having sex with people, and overall I am doing pretty well." If anyone ever asked him if he was a believer he would reply, "Yeah, I invited Jesus into my heart when I was little," and then the matter would be left alone.

This all changed when one day at church Matt heard the pastor's sermon on the first four verses of Ephesians chapter two. "And you were dead in your trespasses and sins," the pastor had begun. "Meaning you could do nothing on your own account to save yourself from your horribly lost position in sin." Continuing on with the passage the pastor read, "in which you formerly walked according to the course of this world, according to the prince of the power of the air, of the spirit that is now working in the sons of disobedience."[1]

Looking out into the crowd, the pastor pointed at one side of the room. Moving his hand across the whole auditorium he said, "All of you were born dead in your sins. You could do nothing good! You all lived in line with this world and in line with the prince of the power of the air, who is the devil." That sent a chill down Matt's spine, and he leaned a little forward in his chair as he continued listening. "You were all sons of disobedience, and the devil was your leader. You all constantly lived indulging your flesh and doing what you wanted to do when you wanted to do it." Raising his voice almost to a yell he shouted, "And you were by nature children of wrath!"

Matt's eyes grew wide. He didn't know what all went into being a child of wrath, but he definitely knew it didn't sound good.

The pastor then walked over to the podium, picked up his Bible and began flipping to something. "Romans nine," he said still obviously passionate and still half shouting, "What if God, although willing to demonstrate His wrath and to make His power known, endured with much patience vessels of wrath prepared for destruction."[2]

Walking back across the stage closer to the congregation, he raised his Bible in the air and repeated, "Vessels of wrath prepared for destruction." As he glanced around looking at all those sitting in the church he said, "All of you who have not put your faith in Christ's perfect sinless life, his death on the cross, and his resurrection from the dead are still in your sin. You are still a child of the devil awaiting the wrath of God."

The words "child of the devil" rang in Matt's ears. Fear, starting in his finger tips, spread throughout his body. It had never occurred to him what someone was before they became a child of God.

The rest of the day Matt worried about and contemplated all the pastor had said. If he wasn't a child of God, that would mean he was a child of the devil. An image popped into his mind of him having strings like a puppet, and Satan as a master puppeteer standing above him pulling the strings. The thought of that made him shudder.

Even though Matt prayed occasionally growing up, it was always when he needed something. That night when he went to bed it was a little different for him. He prayed, "God, I don't think I am a child of the devil because I am not that bad. However, I don't think I am your child either. From what the pastor said today, I guess the Bible says I am one or the other. Um," pausing while thinking what to ask, "Please help me figure it all out."

After that prayer Matt went to bed. He was doubtful anything would change; he just wanted the fear he felt that day to go away. However, Matt was about to find out the full extent of the fear he was experiencing.

As Matt drifted off to sleep, he found himself in battle array. He wore a metal, medieval looking helmet, chain mesh shirt, and had a sword at his side. His undershirt and pants were both black.

Once he looked up from his own garb, he noticed that he was surrounded by thousands dressed just like him. He did not recognize any of those around him though. While he was still scanning for familiar faces, they all began to march. Matt, not really knowing what to do, marched along with them.

Matt decided to ask a fellow marcher where they were headed. He looked to his left and without much thought just blurted out, "Where are we going?" The man on his left happened to be a huge, muscular man. He wore no black undershirt beneath his chain mesh yet his whole torso was darkened with tattoos of dragons. The man just glared at Matt and grunted without saying a word. Matt was now definitely more frightened than before. Not only was the man to his left wielding a sword at his side, he also had a large battle ax in his hands. Turning to his right, Matt saw a young teenager who looked about his age. "Do you know where we are headed?" he asked the boy.

"I am going wherever I feel like," the boy said back in a cocky tone.

Matt looked at the teenager as if he was absurd. "Every one of us is going to the same place. Look around us," he said gesturing with his hand to the masses. "We are all marching to the same place."

The boy looked around, shrugged his shoulders and said, "I go where I want to go."

His explanation still didn't seem to make sense to Matt. He could see that everyone around him was obviously going to the same place, and it seemed they were all being led there together.

Just then an angel appeared to the right of the mass of soldiers. The angel was dressed in complete white clothing, and light radiated from it. A voice in Matt's head said, "Attack! He is only here to bind you and take away your freedom. Do not listen to him!" Apparently the mass of soldiers heard the voice in their head as well, because every one that was close to the angel abruptly turned to face it. Several men charge at him with swords drawn and arrows flew through the air towards him, yet still no one or no arrow ever seemed to reach him.

The angel began to speak. His words came booming out of his mouth loud enough for all to hear, "I am not here to harm you. I come to free you. You are all being tricked; you don't actually have freedom! You are just puppets of the evil one. If you want proof all you have to do is look up."

With a poof the angel was gone as fast as he had appeared. As soon as the words "look up" had come out of the angel's mouth, Matt heard the voice in his head practically screaming, "Don't do it! He is full of lies! His leader will bind you and steal all of your freedom!" Because of the fear these words instilled in Matt, he did not look up. Instead, seemingly involuntarily, he began marching again with the rest of the soldiers.

The marching dragged on for a while, but no one seemed to be getting too tired. The entire time they had been on a steady decline though none of them cared because it made the walking easy. A forest stretched along the left side of all those marching, and to the right was a wide open field.

Suddenly, a loud trumpet was heard. All at once angels and men alike appeared on the field. It was if they had been there the whole time but had been invisible to Matt. All of the angels and men were dressed in white. Matt could see their commander also dressed in white and riding on a white horse. He had tan skin, dark hair, and a beard. He rode closer to Matt. Matt and all those around him were now stopped and staring at the field of men and angels. "Children of wrath, children of the Devil, do you not see what awaits you?" the man on the horse began to yell. "I am Jesus, and I offer another way."

"Lies!" screeched the voice in Matt's head, "Keep marching!" But Matt did not keep marching. This time he stood there watching Jesus. The rest of the soldiers around him did begin to march though, and they made standing still very difficult. They all pushed and shoved Matt since he was now in their way.

Jesus once again yelled out, "Look up all of you who are in doubt of who your leader truly is. You think you are free, but you have been deceived by the deceiver himself. You are all My enemies and are headed for My Father's wrath."

Matt finally got the courage to whip his head up to the sky. Above him he saw a frightening scene. It was as if his imaginary thoughts before he went to bed had come to life. Satan himself was literally playing the part of a puppet master. All those marching had strings, and Satan controlled them all.

Matt was terrified. He truly was an enemy of God. Panic began to race through his body as his mind fumbled with ideas of what to do. He began to slowly back away from Jesus while still being pushed by the marching soldiers. After a few seconds, he took off running into the woods to his left. He threw his helmet on the ground as he ran. While trying to unhook his belt to remove his sword, he lost his balance and crashed to the ground. Unhurt, Matt jumped up and took the time to remove the sword and sheath while standing still. Once he removed it, he began to run again in the opposite direction from the soldiers.

"I don't want to be an enemy of God!" he screamed out loud. "I don't want to be destined for God's wrath!" As soon as the words came out of his mouth, Matt realized he had run out of the other side of the woods. He looked around and saw a small stream of water about ten feet from where he stood. Jesus sitting on a rock on the other side of the stream. Jesus' white horse was drinking from the stream and stood at his side.

"Come here," Jesus said to Matt. Matt slowly walked over to him. Jesus put out his hand gesturing at a rock for Matt to sit down on. After Matt took a seat on the rock facing Him, Jesus then asked, "So now you truly see that you have been a son of disobedience and ruled by the prince of the power of the air, Lucifer himself."

"I'll change!" Matt quickly blurted out. "I will do what You command now."

Jesus just shook his head. "There is nothing you can do Matt," he said. "You could never do anything to save yourself from your sin. You are dead in your sins. Can a dead man make himself alive?"

Matt's head hung gloomily. Nothing could be done? It didn't seem right. There had to be something.

"Why do you think I had to die Matt?" Jesus asked.

"You died so that we wouldn't have to go to hell," Matt answered.

"You have heard that growing up your whole life, and you still have never turned to me and actually believed it."

"I do now!" Matt quickly added looking up at Jesus.

Jesus smiled and began to explain things in more detail to Matt. "You see Matt; so many people are just like you. They have heard the gospel their whole life but don't fully grasp what it means. If I were to ask an average professing believer why he put his faith in me, he would say, 'So I don't have to go to hell.' If I then asked why he would have gone to hell he would say, 'For my sin.' Those are both true, but it goes way beyond that. Most people don't understand why they would go to hell for their sin. They don't understand that My Father is a perfect, holy being and can have zero sin in His presence. They don't understand that sin can never be in His presence because He is so holy. Therefore, mankind's sin makes it impossible for them to ever be in the presence of My Father. They are completely unable to do anything to make it possible for My Father to be around them. My Father cannot be in the presence of sin, and mankind is nothing but individual sin factories now."

Matt thought about all Jesus was saying. The verse in Romans finally made sense to him, "There is none righteous, not even one; there is none who understands, there is none who seek for God; all have turned aside, together they have become useless; there is none who does good, there is not even one."[3] 'No amount of good can change the fact that my body is constantly producing sin,' Matt thought to himself, 'Therefore I can't have a relationship with God.' This thought made him shake his head and look towards the ground.

"Man also doesn't understand that my Father is just," Jesus said. "He is completely perfect and can do nothing that is unjust. At the creation of the world, My Father told Adam that if he sinned he would surely die not only a physical death but a spiritual death as well. That meant that man would be separated from My Father here on earth because of sin, and when man died he would be forever separated from My Father for eternity. My Father would be acting unjustly if He did not give each sinner the punishment they deserved.

"That is why I had to come," Jesus continued after a short pause. "I had to come to earth to live a sinless life. As God's Son I became flesh and was the first to live My entire life without sinning once. Therefore, I did not deserve to die like the rest of mankind, but I freely chose to give My life as a sacrifice for all of those who do deserve to pay the punishment for their sin."

Jesus quoted a passage from Romans. "'Destruction and misery are in their paths, and the path of peace they have not known. There is no fear of God before their eyes.'[4] Matt you were just on the path to destruction and misery earlier today. If I hadn't come to you, then you would have continued on that path. All those around you had no fear of Me or My Father." Jesus once again quoted a paraphrase from Romans, 'For while you were still helpless, at the right time I died for the ungodly. For My Father and I demonstrated Our love towards you, in that while you were still a sinner, I died for you. Now being justified through My blood you shall be saved from the wrath of My Father.'[5] I died to restore you to a relationship with My Father. You never could have restored the relationship on your own because of your sin."

Matt then awoke from his dream. He understood his lost position and that he was currently headed for the wrath of God. He was afraid of being a child of the devil and did not want to spend life after death apart from God. Realizing he could do nothing on his own to change his standing with God, he got out of bed. Although he knew he didn't need to be on his knees, he knelt down showing his reverence for God. Matt declared his faith in all Christ had told him, and he thanked the Lord for saving him from a lifetime and eternity spent without God.

The next couple years Matt's life began to change. He began to go to youth group more and even enjoyed it. He tried to read in God's Word almost every day and strived to live how God would want him to. Before he graduated from high school, he had gone on two missions trips: one to Central America and the second to Africa. Although his life was definitely not perfect, Matt was excited about now being a child of God.

<u>VERSE REFRENCES</u>

1) **Ephesians 2:1-2**
2) **Romans 9:22**
3) **Romans 3:11-12**
4) **Romans 3:16-18**
5) **Romans 5:6-10**

CHAPTER TWO

Now fifteen years after coming to Christ on his knees, Matt lay motionless in his warm bath water. With his head laid back, he stared at the dull white ceiling. The bathroom fan filled the air with a white noise drowning out any noises that might have been heard otherwise.

He was glad to be secluded from the unrest in his life while soaking in the water and trying to relax. Yet he could not even rest his brain while in the bath. He had things to do around the house like wash the dishes and do a load of laundry before his wife got home from class, but Matt didn't have the motivation to do anything. He felt guilty for laying in the tub trying to relax. All he wanted to do was to enjoy his life like he once did, to be infatuated with his beautiful wife, and to take pleasure once again in all God had given him. But for some reason he couldn't.

For years now Matt had struggled off and on with depression. It had started in his first year of college with feelings of being alone and doubts that anyone would truly ever love him. He had grown up with Christian parents that always told him that they loved him, but he never felt loved or cared about. He had always felt like they only loved him because they did not know the true him. He had grown up feeling that beneath the surface of his life he had qualities that somehow made him unlovable.

Matt had always thought that getting married would take away this hardship, and when he first met his wife to be he was content for awhile. She brought a sense of security to his life and became a source of confidence for him. He had enjoyed his job, his fiancé at the time, his fellowship with friends from church, and his time with God. Then slowly he began to struggle again at times, falling back into one week, two weeks, one month, or longer bouts of depression. Every time it seemed to creep back out of the blue. He never really knew why the depression would come on, and he did not know how to make it go away. Matt would sometimes feel as if his body was made of lead. Trying to make himself get out of the bed in the morning would consist of talking himself through the question now commonly known to him, "What's the point?"

Whenever he had one of his depressive episodes, his daily life became more of a struggle. During these episodes he could not remember the last time he felt any pleasure or even if he ever truly had experienced it. Many times his mind would run wild with fears of losing those close to him, feelings of not being accepted, feelings of not being loved, and a fear that he would struggle with this depression for his entire life. He always attempted to get comfort from the Word of God as he would deal with these difficult times, but many times it just seemed as if he was reading empty words. He constantly prayed that God would take away these difficult times forever. Yet no matter how long he might go without the struggles resurfacing, they always seemed to make themselves known again.

As he laid there in the tub, more and more discouraging thoughts began to emerge to the forefront of his mind. His job seemed pointless, his wife's love seemed empty, he felt unlovable, he felt like a failure for having these struggles, and any light at the end of the tunnel seemed forever out of reach. Year after year he had struggled with loneliness longing for the day he would be married. Now that he had the beautiful wife he always longed and prayed for, he just lay in a bathtub trying to wrap his mind around what went wrong. He had thought his wife would have been the answer he needed and so desperately wanted. He now had a love promised to him until death, but it did not bring the security and absence of depression that he so longed it would.

While laying in the tub he began to pray. "Lord, I don't understand why I feel the way I do. I want to love you, I want to love my wife the way you command me, but I just can't. I try to love her, but I feel it isn't real love. I don't know what it feels like to love, and I don't feel loved. God I don't even understand the point to my life right now. My job is just a meaningless task I do solely to provide money for my wife and I. All of my friends at church seem to evaluate me making it hard to ever want to go to small group anymore. I want you to come back Lord, because this life is too difficult. God, I will probably struggle off an on with depression for the rest of my life. Please help me."

After praying Matt got out of the water and finished some of the things he needed to do around the house. Not long into that he decided that he would just go to bed even though his wife hadn't gotten home yet.

Matt woke up the next morning to the usual repetitive sound of his wife's alarm clock. Every morning he and his wife would both get up at seven to get ready for the day. His wife would take a shower and freshen up in the bathroom while Matt would make their daily breakfast of oatmeal. Ever since his doctor had told him he had high cholesterol, his wife insisted that they eat oatmeal for breakfast every morning. To make it bearable, he would always add a little pour of vanilla extract, a dash of cinnamon, a small handful of raisins, and an arguably overabundance of brown sugar. It was also his daily duty to grind and prepare the coffee for them both.

Mornings were one of the few times a day Matt got to spend time with his wife. As soon as they finished their breakfast, Matt's wife Michelle would be off to work. Michelle worked full time as an office assistant and went several nights a week to college classes attempting to finish her degree in social work. Matt, on the other hand, had worked as a network consultant for three years now. However, six months ago his company had put the majority of their workers on what they called an alternative to large scale lay offs. Now his job consisted of working full time for two weeks and then having two weeks off. This plan allowed his company to keep all their employees, but it was far from an ideal for those trying to provide for a family.

Matt had realized early on in the part time layoffs that God was still providing for him and his wife. They made enough to pay all of their bills, eat well, and still get to go out to eat as well as to the movies occasionally. However, not working as much as Michelle had began to put a strain on him. He would feel worthless during the weeks he didn't work. He read a lot of books, would fix things around the house, and do most of the chores that his wife had done before. Doing all these things still didn't keep thoughts from creeping in his head that a 'real man' would be able to find more work. These thoughts made him feel undeserving of her love and brought up past thoughts of somehow just being unlovable.

As Michelle left for the day, a concerned gaze seeped out of her eyes towards Matt. He knew she could always tell when he was down, and she would always want to help. Most of the time this wouldn't benefit him much though, because he wanted to learn how to get out of and stop these depressive episodes on his own. He felt like getting help was just admitting he was unable to take care of the problem himself. Michelle had many times suggested going to a Christian counselor, but to him that seemed to be admitting he did have something wrong with him that he was unable to deal with. He had also never been a fan of the idea of medicines for depression, so he had always avoided those as well.

As soon as she walked out the door, Matt's brain began to pile on the usual thoughts. "You are worthless and you will never get over this. If you were a real man, you would be able to snap out of it. It is your fault and your sin that keeps you in this depressive mood." The last thought was the one that hurt the most. He had heard a couple times from well meaning friends that depression is just a symptom of sin. In one of his small group meetings from church, one of the guys had once said, "Anyone living with depression has to be living in known sin." Yet another one of the wives in the group argued back by telling them that her brother was depressed for years but with medicine he had gotten better. To her that proved that it was strictly a biological issue. Matt had just sat there silently during the conversation not wanting his secret struggle with depression to be known.

Most days now Matt would mope around and dwell on these helpless and degrading thoughts as his mind would be bombarded with one thought after another. But this day was going to be different he told himself. Matt decided to do some yard work. He had been planning on finishing a stone patio for awhile now but never got around to doing it.

He headed outside and began to look through the pile of large rocks which were in a heap in the yard. Attempting to match them up to those already laid, he began thinking about his prayers the last few days. Would God answer him? Would he recover from this off and on depression?

In almost no time at all, he had already laid enough stones to enlarge the patio by a foot. It was now about six feet long and four and a half feet wide. He wanted his finished product to be a ten by ten patio. His wife had wanted one ever since they moved into their house. So this looked like a good way to use his free time off of work to please Michelle. As he continued working, he began to hope that when Michelle got home she would notice how much he had accomplished. He stepped back a minute to admire his work. After admiring it he started sorting through the stones to find which one he would put in place next.

Matt had only been sorting through the stones about two minutes when he began to get a sharp pain shooting down his left arm. He stopped working for a second and made a fist and released it. He looked down at his arm as the pain continued to pulse through it. He thought, "Oh no! I am having a heart attack!" His heart began to race as soon as that thought popped into his mind. He began to gasp for air because it felt as if his lungs were now closing. Fears that he could be dying began to race through his mind, and he started to panic.

He rushed over to his neighbor's house. His neighbor, Harold, an older single man, realized there was a problem as soon as he opened the door. He grabbed his keys quickly without asking any questions and led Matt to his truck. "I am going to drive you to the hospital. Try to settle down, alright? What's going on?"

Matt could hardly reply through his gasps for air. He felt as if he was surely dying. His hands and arms felt numb, he felt lightheaded, and he was shaking. His heart was still pounding upon arriving at the emergency room.

Once inside the hospital, a nurse escorted Matt into a room right away. Being at the hospital had calmed him down quite a bit, but he was still very frightened by what had happened. He explained his symptoms first to the nurse and also to the doctor when he came in. Several tests were run, but the doctor told him, "There is nothing wrong with you. It is possible that you pinched a nerve in your back while working and that sent the pain down your arm. The rest of your symptoms can be explained by a panic attack."

Matt had a quiet ride home with his neighbor. His thoughts were all over the place. He thanked his neighbor Harold for the ride and then headed into his own house. Discouragement of all kinds seemed to pile on him as soon as he walked into his house. Should he call Michelle? He knew if he called his wife she would worry enough to come home. Also, he felt the embarrassment for how large a reaction he had had for something so insignificant. He had never had a panic attack before. Would he have one again? Matt laid down on the couch, and after several minutes of fighting off discouraging thoughts he finally fell asleep.

After Matt drifted off to sleep, he found himself sitting on a log next to Michelle. There were actually a bunch of his friends sitting on logs surrounding a roaring camp fire. Several tents were scattered around them, and trees enclosed their camp site on every side. As Matt scanned the faces of those around the fire, he began to recognize all of them. There were some of his coworkers, some friends from church, one of his brothers, a couple guys he used to work out with, and his wife. They were all laughing and seemed to be having a fantastic time. Matt just sat silently as his eyes roamed from person to person. Even though he was surrounded by close friends and family, he felt surprisingly alone. 'No one seems to be looking at me; no one seems to notice me. Maybe if I say something they will,' he thought. He opened his mouth to say something and stared at all the laughing faces. "I have nothing to say though," he thought as he dejectedly closed his mouth. He stood up, and no one seemed to notice. So he turned and walked away.

Matt looked over his shoulder a couple times as he walked away, but none of his friends moved from the ring around the fire. He turned and began to walk up a path going into the dark woods. There was barely enough moonlight poking through the trees to reveal the course of the path. As he zigzagged his way through the trees, Matt got further and further away from the clearing. The further into the woods he got, the more various noises he began to hear. Each noise was different, but all were equally frightening to him. At one point he even heard a wolf howl in the distance. The sound of that made his head whip back and forth quickly as he tried to detect the direction in which it came from. After walking for awhile, Matt came across a lake.

He walked up to the edge of the water and took a seat in the dirt. The moon seemed to be the only light coming from the sky that night. All of the stars were shining bright but did not illuminate the water in front of him like the moon. Peering across the water, Matt could not see where the lake ended and the forest began. The trees themselves just looked like pure darkness; the only thing that distinguished them as trees were the tops of a few that towered over the others as moonlight shone through their tops accenting their branches.

While Matt was observing his surroundings, he heard a loud 'snap!' behind him. He jerked his head around and saw a tall old man coming towards him out of the woods. When the moonlight hit the man's face, Matt noticed his features. He had a larger than average nose, deep set eyes, a grey neatly trimmed beard which accented his grey head, and an abnormally big smile. "Hey Matt!" the man yelled to him as he walked out of the woods. The man then came over and plopped down next to him.

"Do I know you?" Matt responded with a curious look on his face.

"Well of course you do! I am you, just an older version that's all," the old man replied.

Matt smirked at the man and said, "Well apparently I am not very attractive at an old age." At that comment the old man roared with laughter for a minute or two.

After older Matt pulled himself out of his laughing frenzy, his demeanor suddenly changed. His thick eyebrows scrunched together and he said, "So what are you doing out here alone when all those you care about are having fun at the fire?"

Matt just kept his eyes fixed on the water in front of him for awhile. After a long silence, he sighed and replied, "I don't know. They didn't seem like they wanted me there."

The older man shook his head and said, "That is just how you feel. What proof do have that they don't want you there?"

Matt quickly shot back with, "Uh, well I can tell! You know it is possible to be able to tell when you are wanted or not."

Older Matt once again just slowly shook his head and said, "Yes it is possible, but a conclusion like that also requires some factual evidence. All you have are assumptions and thoughts. Just because you feel like something is true doesn't make it true. All you arc doing is allowing your emotions and thoughts to control your life!"

Memories of various situations began to pour through his mind verifying older Matt's last statement. Many times he had been disabled by his mood, and his emotions were definitely not always based on truth. Matt remembered several occasions that he had let his mood control an entire day. One day in particular, he had gotten up dreading going to work. A coworker named Jake had made a comment the day before that made Matt irate. 'Jake is probably going to say this today,' Matt had thought. Then he began to formulate what he would say back. After five minutes he had already produced a fake conversation with Jake and was now even more upset at him. That entire day Matt had been stressed, tense, and unwilling to even talk to Jake. From morning till evening, Matt's anger had controlled his mood, what he thought about, and his actions. Right before he left work that evening, he overheard Jake talking to another coworker. Matt realized that he had just misunderstood Jake the day before.

Matt continued reminiscing through several memories of when he had let his emotions control him when older Matt interrupted his thoughts by asking, "How do you think these controlling emotions affect your relationships?"

"Well, it's not good," Matt hopelessly asserted. "I know it doesn't help, but that doesn't make it any easier to change. It is how I have always been. My mood just drags me down sometimes, and no matter how hard I try I can't change that. When I feel unloved and alone, I just can't make myself snap out of it."

Old Matt responded after a short pause, "True, but there is still a huge difference between being unloved and feeling unloved. You are just going to have to learn to change your thinking patterns. It will be hard and will take time, yet it is not impossible."

Matt stared once again across the lake into the dark forest as he pondered that statement. Every time he thought about saying something, he just shook his head and continued his gaze. After several minutes of silence, Matt asserted with a helpless tone, "So how do I change?"

The old man looked compassionately at Matt and replied, "You need to find that answer in the Bible."

"I have tried that, and.."

Older Matt cut him off by saying, "Let me finish." Matt rolled his eyes and began to listen.

"You realized at a young age that you were a sinner unable to come to God on your own account; you realized that Jesus' death and resurrection paid the penalty for your sin; and you realized that believing this truth gave you eternal life and a personal relationship with God Almighty. Ever since then you have put all of your hope for life after death in Him and in His word, but what about your life now?" This got Matt's attention, and he turned and listened intently to his older self. "You came to Christ on your knees knowing your need of Him. Now you come to His word looking for answers to your problems. You try to find verses that will tell you how you can change."

Matt perked up, "Yeah, that's what I have been taught to do."

"I know that is what you have been taught, but you don't come to the word wanting anything more than a formula. You want to put in the minimum amount of time, find an encouraging verse, and be on your way." Matt saw the truth in what his older self was saying. Older Matt continued on, "I know you pray and ask God to help you change, but it ends there for you. The Word of God says as you have received Christ Jesus the Lord, so walk in Him.[1] You received Christ by faith and only by faith! You understood and now still understand that you need Him as a savior. When you come to the place where you admit your need of Christ for daily living with practical things like your emotions, mood, and actions, then the Word of God will teach you how to change."

Matt's eyes focused on the water and darkness before him. He was realizing the truth to the words being spoken. Older Matt continued, "You want so badly to fix all your own problems. You strive everyday to earn the love of your wife which she gives you so freely. You do the same with God too. You want to be dependent on no one and you don't want help from anyone. Why do you think your subconscious brought an older version of yourself to you? It's because even your brain knows deep down that you wouldn't listen to anyone else."

Matt let out a sigh as his eyes dropped from his forward gaze down to his lap. He didn't know when his older self had left, but when he finally looked up, he was alone once again.

VERSE REFRENCES

1) **Colossians 2:6**

CHAPTER THREE

Matt awoke from his dream still lying on his couch. It had now been a couple hours since he had arrived home from the hospital after his panic attack. He reached over and grabbed his Bible which was sitting on the coffee table. Rolling onto his back, he began to read. After about five minutes of reading, he remembered that he hadn't prayed before he began. He quickly said, "God I know I need help, but I don't know how to receive it. Give me understanding of what You're trying to say to me through Your word." With that he opened his Bible back up and continued reading through the Psalms.

He was amazed by how open and honest David had been with God. Matt read and read, yet he still never had the epiphany that he was hoping for. After reading about an hour, he put down his Bible and headed to the kitchen. As he prepared dinner, discouraged feelings began to loom over him again. Once again he had come away from reading the Bible without feeling encouraged or getting an answer on what to do differently.

Michele arrived home that night as Matt was putting the food on the table. She came in and gave him a big hug while asking, "How was your day?"

Immediately Matt felt the Holy Spirit tug on his heart saying, "You remember how open and honest David was in the Psalms? That is what I wanted to teach you today through my Word. Be open and honest to her! Tell her what happened today, tell her your struggles, tell her your worries, and tell her your pain! She loves you and wants to help you."

Matt instead made a joke about his struggles that day. "So I thought I was having a heart attack today. I went to the emergency room, but they just called me a faker and sent me home!" he said with a little laugh.

The rest of dinner was spent with Michele asking a bunch of concerned questions about what had happened. Matt told her that the doctors had said it was most likely a panic attack, but that he didn't know why he would have had one. It was probably nothing and shouldn't be worried or stressed over he told her.

Deep inside he knew that there was more to the story; he just wasn't ready to open up. Matt was not even that afraid of her response. He was just afraid of telling her his struggles.

The rest of the night Matt and Michele spent together watching the news, Wheel of Fortune, and then a movie that they got from Netflix. Every now and then during the evening, Matt got bombarded with negative thoughts like, 'You are such a pansy for not telling her!' and 'You will always be afraid.' After the movie was over, they both sleepily headed to bed.

This is the part of the story that I come in. You see, after Matt had the dream mentioned last chapter, he began to realize a lot about the way he lived his life. He realized, ironically through talking to an older version of himself in a dream, that getting some assistance from others might help him deal with his struggles.

Some background to Matt's struggles goes back to a few years after he had gotten saved. He had enjoyed the excitement and peace of becoming a new believer, but as months grew to years, it waned and faded away. After receiving his salvation from hell, he felt as if he was given a list of things he had to do now: honor your father and mother, don't steal, don't lie, as so on. Since then he has realized how hard it is to not sin. His desire to sin didn't leave after he trusted in Christ, and life was a struggle for him as it is with every other Christian. His pride did not just go away and neither did his other bad habits.

This all set the stage for his more recent struggles. He felt it was his duty and responsibility to do good, stop sinning, and through those things make himself pleasing to God. He developed the mindset that failure and giving into sin at any time just meant he had to try harder. This battle raged on in Matt's heart for years, but he never opened up about it. All other Christians he encountered did not seem to have the struggles he had. They all appeared to have their lives in order and never shared any struggles with sin. This caused Matt to feel like he alone struggled with this issue and it was his fault. Therefore, the logical explanation to him was that he had to recover from this himself. He felt he had to do it all alone and saw asking for help as a sign of weakness.

Matt's dream influenced him enough that he decided to come see me. I am a licensed Christian counselor and have been doing this now for a little over eight years. Throughout the years I have talked with and counseled a wide variety of people. With the Lord working through me, I have helped many of them work through a lot of issues. Others have come to see me for months and remained in the same lousy condition they arrived. It is always very difficult at first to read the people that come to see me. Some come because a spouse wants them to. Others come because they are hurting, depressed, fearful, or just struggling with an issue of some sort. It usually takes me a few sessions to see if the person actually wants to put forth effort to change or if they are just at counseling to say they tried it. Sometimes people come for the sole purpose of pouting and complaining to me about all the hard things God has allowed into their life.

Those people never had any desire to change or grow; they just wanted someone to feel sorry for them.

Matt, on the other hand, was different from the beginning. The first day he met with me, which happened to be the day after his dream, he completely opened up about his struggles. He shared what he was currently going through with depression, his hardships growing up, and all the feelings of worthlessness that he carried around with him. It was obvious that he was hurting, wanted to change, but did not know how.

One aspect that was unusual with Matt's counseling sessions with me was the process of his recovery. Normally in a counseling session, I would begin by asking question after question to get to know the counselee. After establishing some comfort with them, I would begin asking leading questions. For example: 'What about this? Have you ever considered that? Why do you think that hurts so much?' It usually takes a while for a person to break down their hard or hurting heart and begin to let the Holy Spirit work in the areas they are dealing with. Matt did not require this gentle nudging along. He came to me a broken man ready for change. He opened up immediately and bare his heart. The weird thing was, I never actually 'counseled' him; I felt more like a friend encouraging him. At first Matt just told me his struggles, and as he began to grow he would share all God was teaching him. Somehow it just seemed therapeutic for him to learn to open up to others about his struggles.

Another element that was different in my interaction with Matt was when he would tell me about all his dreams. It was very clear that God was using these dreams to speak to him. God seemed to be using dreams to help Matt better understand His Word, and by using them God spoke a lot of truth into Matt's life. This concept was very hard for me at first. I grew up going to a Baptist church although now I don't consider myself a Baptist, and I was taught that God does not communicate through dreams anymore. At the

Christian College I attended, I was taught to be very skeptical of those claiming God was speaking to them through dreams. Even though Matt's experience has opened my mind to God's various ways of working, I still believe it is wise to not blindly believe everyone who claims to hear God's voice into their lives. It was not hard for me to believe Matt's dreams because they were laced with truth. His dreams did not contradict the Word of God, and most of his dreams contained verses from the Bible. I began to see that God was using this way of communication to help Matt understand passages and Bible verses that he had read in the past.

Matt only came to counseling sessions for about a month, but during that time we grew to be close friends. It was amazing to see the Lord work in his life and to watch him grow.

Although Matt no longer comes to counseling sessions, he still comes back to see me from time to time. On a recent visit to me, he came in with an old tattered notebook rolled up in his hand like a newspaper. After we caught up on things going on in our lives, he handed me the notebook. He said it contained all the dreams he had during that first month we met. It also contained his struggles at the time and what God had taught him through the various dreams.

"I want others who may struggle with the same things that I do to know they aren't alone. I would be overjoyed if God used my story to help others grow closer to the Lord," he told me.

This book is Matt's story. He gave me permission to tell other clients about his recovery and struggles and to even write this book if I thought it would encourage others. All that follows in the pages to come is either exerts from his journal or supplemental information I remembered from our sessions together. Whenever a verse is referenced or quoted in one of Matt's dreams, I put an endnote following the chapter so you could look it up if you wanted to. I pray God uses Matt's story to speak to you as well as to help you grow closer to our Lord.

But getting back to the story, this was the day when Matt and I first met. After Michele had left for work, he happened to find my name in the yellow pages while looking for a counselor. Normally I wouldn't have openings the first day someone called me, but that day I had just had someone cancel their late morning appointment.

Matt arrived about a half an hour early for his appointment. He had a larger than average nose, eyes that had a serious appearance, perfectly trimmed stubble, and short black hair that was spiked in the front. When I invited him into my office, he entered and walked over and sat down on the love seat. I followed him to one of the two chairs facing him and also took a seat. He put his feet up on the edge of the coffee table and began to open up before I said a word. He shared all that was going on in his life and how he wanted to open up to Michele but couldn't bring himself to do it.

He talked for around forty minutes without me interjecting anything. His story finally ended by him telling me how he had come across my name that morning. He then asked me why he struggled to open up with Michele more. That made me chuckle a little and reply, "That is what I was going to ask you actually!"

After thinking about it a few moments, I asked him if he had ever heard that avoiding problems and emotional hardships is the cause of many psychological disorders and problems. He shook his head no, so I elaborated a little more. "At the very core of a person is the desire to do what he feels is best for him. Everyone wants to be comfortable; nobody wants to experience any more pain or sorrow than they have to. God made our minds respond to discomforts, dangers, or anything that threatens us in a way commonly known as 'flight or fight'. When our mind perceives a threat of some kind, it will naturally try to run from the issue or take the issue head on. These are not only physical threats but also threats to our emotional well being. People don't want to hurt and will do everything in their power to minimize their emotional pain. When a person is presented with an emotionally difficult situation, rather than deal with it and handle the problem face on, many times the person will side step or run from it. Doing this never actually takes away the problem nor does it improve it. Most of the time, it actually makes the problem worse."

Matt responded that he had never really thought about that before and would give it some thought. We shook hands, set up his next appointment time, and he headed home.

When Matt fell asleep that night he found himself slowly walking down a trail next to a swift river. The path was only a foot or so wide, and it curved continually around the bend hugging the river as far as he could see. The only things that separated him from the river were boulders and other large rocks. Both sides of the river were lined with these rocks making the river look extremely fierce. On the other side of the river, the towering evergreen trees seemed to leap out of the ground at the edge of the rocks. The trees were so thick that he couldn't see much further than a few feet into the woods. On the side of the river that he found himself, there was a small strip of knee high grass that separated him from the evergreens. White clouds loomed overhead not letting a single ray of sunlight through although it was still very light out.

Seemingly content, Matt strolled his way down stream on the path. Every now and then, he would throw a stick into the river and watch it swiftly be whisked away. After he had rounded the first big bend in the river, the water began to take on a much more ferocious demeanor. The boulders no longer were just scattered along the banks. They now found themselves sporadically plopped in the middle of the now roaring river.

Matt had just begun to get accustomed to its roar when it began to calm down once again. Even though it had calmed down, he still heard the sound of pounding water up ahead. Probably a waterfall, he thought. Sure enough, as he got closer he saw the river appear to vanish over an edge in front of him. Startled by movement, his eyes focused in on the large object moving in the middle of the river, and he realized he was staring at a black bear. It definitely wasn't very big, but then again no bear could be described as small. As Matt got closer, he noticed the bear was grabbing fish as they jumped up the small waterfall. It was amazing to watch, but Matt did not really want to be standing there in case the bear might get tired of eating fish. So he started walking down the trail once again.

As he rounded another bend in the river, he came across a burly bearded man. He wore a flannel shirt and rubbery fishing pants with suspenders strapped over his shoulders. His hair was close to shoulder length, but its length and unkemptness were far from flattering. He was standing in the now significantly calmer river fly fishing. Matt walked over near him and asked, "How's the fishing today?" The man slowly turned his head towards Matt with a perturbed look on his face as if to say, why are you bothering me? Matt looked down at the water and saw a line with several fish that the man had already caught. "Looks like you definitely know what you're doing!" Matt exclaimed.

The man slightly warmed his expression a bit and glanced back at Matt saying, "Well I better know! I have lived up here so long that I would have been in deep trouble if I couldn't catch some fish."

Matt, a little surprised that someone would live out in the wilderness, said, "How long have you lived up here?"

"I don't know. I didn't ever really want to keep track. I reckon I moved out here about ten years ago."

Matt introduced himself to the man and learned that the man's name was Tom. Matt wanted to laugh a little when he heard the man's name, because it didn't seem to fit. Tom was such an average, normal name. It wasn't what he would expect for a Paul Bunyan looking man living secluded in the wilderness.

After chatting awhile Matt learned a significant amount about Tom. Now that Tom had begun talking about his life, it appeared he would keep on talking forever. Matt didn't mind though; he was enjoying hearing the stories of living in the wilderness. He also discovered that Tom had built a small cabin not far from there.

Once Tom had reached a breathing point after summing up one of his stories, Matt interjected, "Oh, I saw a bear a little ways up the river a while ago."

Tom whipped his head around, eyes large, and said with a scared excitement, "How large was it?"

"Not too big," Matt replied.

"Oh, that is just Desire. But either way, we better get going. Would you want to join me for a salmon dinner?"

Matt nodded yes but quickly replied with, "So um... Did you name that bear Desire?"

As they began walking down stream, Tom began to elaborate the story of how he had named the bear. "You know, Desire is a female bear. I named her and her brother, Abandonment. He is huge and ferocious. He could tear you limb from limb and leave you lying in a pile of agony. He is much more frightening, and I flee for my life whenever he is around. Desire isn't as threatening. Sometimes I even think she wants to play a game with me. Kind of ridiculous isn't it? Like a bear would play fetch with a human or something. Either way, I know it's best if I just stay away from both of them."

Tom now directed Matt with his hand towards a path that now headed into the heart of the woods. Leaving the openness by the river, their path was now much darker. The thick evergreens overhead blotted out much of the daylight. Their path now not only consisted of dirt, but it was also covered with millions of brown pine needles. Puzzled with curiosity Matt asked, "How did you choose those names?"

"Well", Tom began his reply, "I guess that goes back to why I came to the woods in the first place. I used to be married you see. And.."

"You were married?" Matt interrupted.

"Yeah, I was married for nine years before I came up here. I loved my wife, but..." Matt could see the hurt on Tom's face as he tried to put these memories into words. After a short silence, Tom finished his statement, "...but I was always afraid she would leave. I felt I wasn't good enough for her. I feared that I would never be able to love her enough and that I wasn't good enough to deserve her love. Because of that I feared she would leave."

After walking a couple minutes and realizing that Tom wasn't going to say more unless spurred on, Matt asked, "So how did you end up here?"

"I just left one day." Tom's remorse could be heard in his response. "I couldn't take it anymore. Wondering if she was going to leave me drove me to leave. I didn't know where to go. I just knew I wanted to get far away from everyone. I felt like she would be better off without me, as if I dragged her down or something. So I wandered out here and never went back."

"So, well, do you ever think about going back? Do you ever think about your wife?" Matt tried to ask cautiously making sure not to offend his new companion.

"Of course I do, but I just force those thoughts out. Why would I want to think about something that brings me pain? Leaving didn't take away the worries and fears like I hoped it would. I just have to force myself to never think about them now."

Tom paused for a moment and looked as if he was in deep thought. After the pause he said, "The first time I saw the huge ferocious bear staring me down on the river's edge I ran for my life of course. My fear of the bear was so intense, I decided to name him after the biggest fear of my life, Abandonment."

Nothing was said the next couple minutes as Matt processed the story he just heard. After walking a while longer, he asked, "So why did you name the smaller bear Desire?"

Tom chuckled at this question, which was the first time Matt had seen him smile at all. "Desire isn't too threatening. She has never chased me and hardly ever scares me. She sometimes even makes me smile imagining being able to play a game with her. However, she is a bear, and bears are not tame. You can't control them. That reasoning is how I came to name her Desire. My desires aren't harmful; I would even probably enjoy getting some of the things I want now and then. I once had dreams about how grand my future was going to be, but the fact that no future event is certain and that anything can be cancelled or taken away at any time made me fear getting attached or looking forward to something too much. Desires are just dreams of happiness that will never fulfill and probably never even come true. Ultimately, like a bear, they will end up hurting you."

"So you just run away from all your fears and desires then?" Matt asked a little shocked.

"I always thought life would be easier this way. I don't have to worry about losing anything because I have nothing to lose. If I don't strive to achieve great things, then I can't let myself down."

Matt then asked, "Does it work?"

Tom stopped walking for a second and looked at Matt with empty eyes and replied, "I hurt just as much out here as I did before."

Tom's statement penetrated Matt's heart. Matt could see the pain on Tom's face, and he felt sorry for him. After a silent pause, they began walking again, and Matt asked, "Why don't you just go back then?"

"I can't!" Tom snapped back as he looked at the ground. "It would be too hard, and I don't think my wife would ever take me back. The fear of her leaving me just turned into the fear of her not taking me back once I came out here."

Realizing the gravity and the pain involved in that statement Matt didn't respond. He noticed out of the corner of his eye that Tom momentarily glanced up at the little bit of sky visible through the trees with a certain sense of longing, but when Tom's eyes came back to the trail before him they were glazed with hurt.

The rest of the walk to the cabin was quiet. Neither Matt nor Tom said anything else. Both were busy thinking over their lives. As the cabin was coming into sight, Matt heard a noise. For some reason it didn't seem to fit in his surroundings. It sounded like an alarm. He then woke up to the ringing of his wife's alarm clock .

CHAPTER FOUR

Matt roused himself from bed and made his way to the kitchen to prepare breakfast. He could not stop thinking about his dream and the various struggles the man had talked about. He saw how irrational the thoughts were when someone else was thinking them; yet that did not make it any easier for him to just let his thoughts go. Did he try to avoid emotional pain like Tom had? Matt realized he wouldn't open up to Michele about his troubles because it would be too hard emotionally for him. "I feel that talking about those things will leave me so vulnerable and insecure," he said to himself. He smiled for a second when he remembered what 'old Matt' had said a couple days ago in his dream about acting on feelings, not truth.

Understanding his inadequacy to handle the situation, Matt began to pray, "Lord, I don't know what to do. I don't feel good enough for Michele, and I worry that she might leave me because of all of my problems. I am scared to open up to her because I don't know how she will react. Please give me the courage to talk to her about this kind of stuff."

The day progressed as a normal day for Matt. He ate breakfast with Michele, cleaned up the kitchen, worked on the patio, then laid on the couch and read. The whole day he planned on how he would open up to Michele about his struggles and share how much he had been hurting lately. He was also planning on telling her he had starting counseling. When dinner came that night, it went the same as the evening two nights before. Matt made some small talk with Michele about her day and briefly shared what he had done that day. More than once during their meal Michele asked, "Are you alright? Looks like something is bothering you?"

Matt put on a deceiving smile and denied anything was wrong. He could feel the fear of being vulnerable to her holding him back. He slowly replied, "I just wish I could work more that's all. It's kind of boring not working for two weeks straight."

Michele put her hand on Matt's leg and replied, "I will always will be here and want you to tell me when things are bothering you alright? I love you."

"I love you too," Matt responded.

As he got up and began clearing the table, degrading thoughts began to bombard him. 'If you truly loved her you would open up to her! You know you can't open up to her because she probably won't love the real you. She will be sick of hearing about the pain and anguish that you invent for yourself. Men don't struggle with emotional issues like this. You are a terrible husband if you are more emotional than your wife.' After just a minute of washing dishes, it became a struggle not to just scream in an attempt to get the thoughts to end. He turned on the radio to try to see if that would help at all.

About that time Michele left for the evening to head to her class. Matt's eyes almost began to tear up as soon as she left. The negative thoughts were now the only thoughts circling in his mind. The general consensus of them all: 'You are worthless.' He wished he would have opened up to Michele. Matt knew that she would have skipped her class that evening to be with him if he had just asked. "If she would have skipped her class for me, that would mean my emotional problems were interrupting and setting her life back," Matt dejectedly said to himself.

Matt only got half way through doing the dishes before he finally gave in and quit. "What's the point?" he asked himself. He went and filled up a warm bath, turned on the bathroom fan, and slid into the water.

Once again he found himself staring at the dull white ceiling. He still could not escape his racing negative thoughts. A few tears ran down his cheeks as he felt like this pain would never leave. "God, I can't do this much longer. Please help me," was the only prayer he could voice.

Still being beat down by his thoughts and unable to put them at bay, Matt decided to take some Nyquil and head to bed even though it was only eight p.m. He didn't want to be up when Michele got home because it hurt to think about having to admit to her all the thoughts and emotions that controlled his mind all evening. 'She wouldn't understand and possibly wouldn't accept me if she knew all my struggles. She might even leave me,' were the excuses his brain gave him. He laid his head down on his pillow and once again let a few tears fall. He knew he needed to open up, but it just seemed too hard. While drifting off to sleep, in despair he prayed, "God, I need you more than ever! I can't do this anymore. I can't live like this." He then fell asleep.

Matt now found himself in a thick, exotic jungle. There were palm trees growing all around and thick trees that towered over top. Vines stretched from the ground to branches far above. The undergrowth produced walls of green on every side of him. The bushes and trees prevented Matt from seeing any farther than twenty feet in any direction. At his feet lay a small dirt path only about a foot wide. It was obvious that it was only ever taken by animals or humans, because any motor vehicle would have widened the path.

After the few short seconds that it took Matt to scan his surroundings, he realized that he was naked. The shock and surprise paralyzed him for a second. Even though he was in the middle of a jungle, he still felt the fear of being nude while not in the comfort of his home. 'What if someone else comes walking down this path?' he frantically thought. He immediately began searching for some big leaves in an attempt to make some quick clothes. He found a couple big bushes nearby which grew some rather large leaves. He pulled many of them off the bushes and then searched for a ropelike vine. Most of the vines growing around him were pretty thick, but he did manage to find one small enough that he could bend and form it. Matt then poked the vine through the leaves he had picked.

The whole process did not seem to take very long, and it left Matt with a leaf covering which he tied around his waist. He thought it looked very similar to a rudimentary grass skirt and still did not want to run into anyone along the trail.

Being partially covered now only reduced Matt's vulnerable feeling slightly, but since he was at least partially dressed now, he began walking down the trail. The path curved its way through the jungle and split into two separate paths multiple times. After walking for a while, Matt felt like he was possibly walking in circles. The dense jungle made it hard to distinguish which way he had come from and which direction he was heading in. Many times he would pass a location and think, 'I swear I have been here before,' but after a minute of standing there, he would just continue walking.

Once again coming up to a split in the trail, Matt heard a voice in the distance. He quickly began to panic. All of the fears of being seen half nude stirred once again inside of him. 'I have to hide!' his mind screamed at him as he began to veer off the trail. His walk turned into a jog and then into a quick sprint. The bushes were now scraping against his body as he ran straight into the wild jungle. Several branches painfully smacked his face. After getting hit one too many times by the branches, Matt decided to settle at the distance he had gone.

He got down on his hands and knees and looked back towards the trail he had run from. He sat there a couple minutes but saw no one. Just when he was about to get up and head back to the trail, he heard a voice once more. It was not coming from the trail he ran from though; it was coming from behind him. All the hair on his body began to stand straight up as he slowly turned around. The voice was still a little muffled, and he still could not see where it came from. Suddenly, a head appeared from around a bush around fifteen feet away. It was a girl who looked like she was in her late teen years. He could only see her neck and head over all of the underbrush. As he tensed up and waited for her companion to come around the bush Matt realized she was alone. The girl was apparently talking to herself. She walked much slower than Matt had been when he was on the trail. "No one can see me like this. I have to keep hiding. If anyone sees me like this my life is over," the girl said out loud. She continued to talk to herself as she slowly made her way through the jungle. "I can't go back to the trail. It was too frightening. Just keep a close eye out for people, and you will be fine," once again voicing her thoughts.

Matt realized she posed no threat to him but did not want to frighten her. So he continued to stay in his hiding position until well after she has passed by.

As he sat there, he began to feel sorry for the girl. Even though he could only see her neck and head, he could still see how tense she had been. He remembered his own insecurities while looking down at the leaf belt he had made as a covering. Feeling pity for the girl, Matt started to say a prayer. "Jesus, I just want to ask You to comfort that girl. Allow her to find comfort in You. And Lord..."

Before he could finish his thought, a man suddenly appeared next to him. The man had dark, thick hair, a medium length beard, and tan skin. Matt still had his mouth hanging open after being abruptly interrupted by the man appearing. "Yes?" the man said to Matt while his mouth still hung open in slight shock.

"Yes... what?" Matt responded.

"You were about to say something else to Me before I appeared to you," the man stated simply.

"Oh, so You are.." was all Matt could reply. Thoughts began to come back to him of his dream in high school. He remembered seeing Jesus on His white horse as well as talking to Him by the stream.

"Jesus." The man replied back with a smile.

Matt quickly straightened his leaf clothing to make sure he was completely covered. "Well, I was just going to ask You to comfort the girl I saw."

"I will Matt; I always look after my children," Jesus answered. He continued, "But right now I want to talk with you Matt. You are equally scared as that young girl. You chose to hide your insecurity instead of dwell on it like she was doing."

Matt first looked down at the leaf clothing he had made and then glanced over to the man. "You're right, I guess. I did try to cover up my nakedness. Who wouldn't though?"

Jesus' eyes seemed to concentrate on Matt's face as he answered, "You know what? You remind me of a couple people I know. You have probably heard of them. Their names are Adam and Eve. You know, the first humans on earth?"

Matt let out a little laugh. "Of course I have heard of them. Everyone has!" Matt said.

Jesus smiled and continued, "I created them naked, and they didn't mind. They never even noticed that they were naked until sin entered the world."

Matt interrupted, "So sin causes people to feel uncomfortable for being naked?"

Jesus replied, "No, sin causes man to be preoccupied with himself. You see Matt, before man sinned he was completely satisfied with My Father. Man looked to Him for everything. In My Father man found his worth, his value, his meaning, and his acceptance. He found it all in Him. Picture Adam and Eve standing in the garden just looking to My Father for everything. They were joyous and content. They had a peace like nothing else. When they sinned their eyes were immediately pulled from Him and cast down at their own bodies. They experienced worry for the first time. Fear raced through their veins as their hearts sped up with never before experienced emotions. They felt the need to hide from My Father, because they no longer felt the comfort and security coming from Him. Adam was unwilling to take his eyes off his own body and his own sin. Frightened, he hid and made clothes for himself. He knew he was unworthy to be in My Father's presence because of his sin. He knew his sin would affect his standing with his God, and so he ran."

Matt considered what was said for a few seconds and responded, "I don't understand how that applies to me right now. I made clothes because I am naked not because I just sinned."

"No, you made clothes because you are insecure Matt. You needed to cover yourself up because you are petrified of being vulnerable in any situation. Adam and Eve could roam the Garden of Eden nude because they confidently knew that they had a right standing before My Father. They knew that He accepted them, loved them, cared for them, and would always be there for them. As soon as they ate from the tree, they were scared to death because they knew He was still righteous, and they now knew that they were not. Matt, that is where you currently are. You are frightened because you feel no one accepts you as you are. Your whole life you have tried to cover up all your imperfections and make your life seem like you have everything under control. However, you are daily struggling with pain, feelings of worthlessness, and no matter how much pain you feel, you are unable to open up to your wife for fear she might not accept you. You run around in your leaf clothing looking for bigger leaves to cover up more of you. In reality, it is just your way of covering up your faults and trying to forget that you feel unlovable."

Matt looked away from Jesus and stared at the ground. He realized all Jesus had told him was completely true. He knew Jesus was still looking deep into his eyes, but Matt didn't want to make eye contact with him. He tried to respond more than once, but every time he opened his mouth to speak no words came to mind.

"I want you to know that I love you Matt," Jesus began again. "And until you are satisfied with My love and acceptance, you will never be secure with who you are. Your fears of sharing your struggles with Michele stem from the fact that you don't feel secure in that relationship. A huge problem though is that you are not supposed to find your security, comfort, and validation from that relationship. You can only find that from My Father and Me."

Matt awoke from his dream well rested long before Michele's alarm clock went off. He decided to head out to the living room, get some coffee, and read. Once the coffee was done brewing, he sat down on the couch and opened up his Bible. Thinking about where to read that morning, he remembered hearing that Ephesians talks a lot about all God had done for us. He flipped to Ephesians and began to read.

Verses four through six seemed to pull at his heart a little; so he backtracked and began to read them again. "Just as he choose us in Him before the foundation of the world, that we should be holy and without blame before Him in love, having predestined us to adoption as sons by Jesus Christ to Himself, according to the good pleasure of His will, to the praise of the glory of His grace, by which He made us accepted in the Beloved."[1] Reading these verses again and again, Matt began to realize what they were saying. Before the world was created, God had decided that all those who believed on Christ would be seen as "in Christ." God would no longer look at their sin tainted lives and bodies, but He would look at Christ's blood and Christ's perfect life. God would now see all those who trust in Christ as being holy and without blame because they were in Christ..

Verse six also began to tug at Matt's heart as he read it again. He felt like it was saying to him that at the highest point of God's grace towards him, God chose to view him as accepted because of the work of Christ.

For the first time, Matt began to realize that once he believed in Christ's finished work on the cross, God no longer viewed him as a sinner in need of punishment. God now views him through the eyes of Christ, meaning that God chooses to look at Christ's righteousness instead of Matt's sin. Matt always knew he could never be acceptable to God on earth because he knew he could never completely stop sinning. But through Christ he is now acceptable to God. Matt realized much more of the magnitude of what Jesus had done for him on the cross. Not only had Jesus saved him from the eternal death waiting for him in hell, He had also made it possible for him to have a relationship with God here on earth based on Christ's righteousness not his own.

As the gravity of these truths began to sink into Matt's mind, a sense of peace started to fall over him. He began to ponder his dream from the night before and realized its direct correlation to these verses. His dream had him wandering around aimlessly worried someone would find him nude and feeling vulnerable. "I look to others for validation and acceptance." Matt said to himself shaking his head as if in disbelief. "I never realized the significance of putting so much emphasis and importance on other's views of me."

Thoughts of Michele popped into Matt's head. Memories began to flood his mind of many instances he had felt unloved by her. The memories began to defog in his brain as he realized the truth behind the feelings. It wasn't that she was being unloving or unkind; it was that he had just felt unlovable and unworthy of her love. He had always thought that getting married would take away those feelings, but now he realized that when he got married he had hoped Michele would fill that huge gap needing love and acceptance he had inside of him. It was as if a light had finally come on in his heart. "I can only find my acceptance from God, and He accepts me solely on the work of His Son." Matt slowly muttered to himself. A peaceful smile came across Matt's face for the first time in a while. This was the first time in as long as he could remember that he felt close with God.

Matt then heard Michele walking down the narrow hall to towards the living room. He glanced over at the clock and saw it read seven thirty. He was surprised by how long he had been out on the couch already and thought that it was strange that he hadn't heard her alarm clock ringing or her taking a shower.

When Michele came around the corner, she was still dressed in the clothes she wore to bed each night. She always wore short grey shorts and a lime green tank top. Matt realized she had not yet gotten ready for the day and questioned why she hadn't.

"It's Saturday," she replied with a smile.

"Oh yeah!" he said back. With that he jumped up, walked over and gave her a hug and a kiss.

"You went to bed really early last night. Were you not feeling well?" asked Michele.

"Yeah, but I am feeling a lot better now," Matt replied with his arm still around her.

Guiding her over to the couch with his arm, they both sat down, and Matt began to open up about his recent struggles and feelings. He told her about his recent fears and how scared he had been to open up. He also shared that he had visited a counselor that week and would be going back on Monday. After he had finished, Michele began to ask a few questions about all he had said. Once it seemed all that needed to be said was out, Michele put her head on Matt's shoulder and her arms around him.

They just sat there a long time enjoying the closeness. A few minutes later Michele looked up at Matt with a huge smile and said, "Let's go out for breakfast!"

VERSE REFRENCES

1) Ephesians 1:4-6 (NKJV)

CHAPTER FIVE

The following Monday was hardly what I had expected. Matt and I had our appointment scheduled for ten a.m. Just as the week before, Matt arrived a half an hour before his appointment was scheduled. When I went to the waiting room to get him, I noticed his downcast appearance. His head hung towards his lap, and it was very obvious he was dejected about something.

After walking into my office, he took the same seat he had taken the week before. His sad eyes met mine, and I knew there would be minimal small talk.

"I lost my job," he told me with a big sigh. Continuing on he told me the whole story. "This morning after Michele left for work I got a call from my boss. He said that our company was downsizing. The temporary lay offs were no longer an option. Corporate was going to be closing down our entire branch, and no one was going to be keeping their job."

"I'm sorry Matt," was all I could say.

Matt faked a small smile and continued on. "It's alright. It is just going to be a lot harder now. I used to feel worthless for not working enough, and now I have no job. The whole time I have been part time laid off I already tried applying to every company in my field within the radius of a forty-five minute drive. I don't know what to do. It is my job as the man to provide for my wife. What am I to do now? I feel like I am becoming a huge failure to Michele."

He filled me in on his dream the following weekend and about how he had opened up with Michele. They had enjoyed a great weekend together, but that all seemed to be eclipsed now by the present situation. After talking a while, we narrowed down his worries and fears into two tangible issues. One was that he was worried about finances. The other was that at his core, like most males, lay the need to provide for his wife. He felt the heavy burden and responsibility that he must provide for her, and if he were to fail, Matt would feel that he was a sub-par man.

When our hour of talking came to an end, not much more seemed to be settled. Matt left my office still downcast, yet now at least he knew what his deeper issues were with losing his job. That evening he shared the news with Michele. They both just sat quietly and cuddled on the couch. Matt turned on the TV after several minutes of silence, and they watched shows the rest of the night. They talked about 'what if' scenarios during the commercials and tried to think up some ideas.

When they realized it was getting late, they both headed to bed. Matt's mind kept going back to the question of how they were going to pay their bills. They had made enough when he at least worked part time, but now he was significantly more worried. How would he provide for his wife? As these thoughts stirred in his mind, he slowly drifted off to sleep.

Matt was now wandering through a large, vast empty field. In the field grew waist high grass that stretched for miles. He walked open palmed with his arms out to his sides watching the blades of grass hit his palms and then slide off. He looked up and peered off into the distance noticing the yellow tint of the grass could be seen for miles. Spinning around in a circle, he realized that it was the same in every direction. Beyond the miles of stretched out field lay mountains. Mountains in every direction enclosed the field. Matt glanced back and forth deciding which way to walk. All the directions looked similar; so Matt decided to continue the direction he thought he had been heading.

As Matt continued to walk, the mountains began to climb higher into the sky and remind Matt, even at a far distance, that these were huge feats to tackle. He began to think about how he would climb the mountain. He had no climbing equipment, nor did he really know the first thing about mountain climbing. Fears began to circle in his head as he tried to think of possible solutions to going over the mountain. It was still an extremely long way off, but he still felt the need to prepare.

The more Matt got concerned with the task of climbing the mountain, the bigger it seemed to get. At first it appeared that it was just his view of it that was growing as he walked closer, but now that didn't seem to be the case. He realized that he was not significantly closer to the mountain, but it definitely appeared to be a lot larger. He once again whirled around in a circle to check the views to the sides and behind him. Those mountains all still seemed the same size as before. Once he rotated a full circle and faced forward again, he still found himself staring at a much larger mountain than it had once been.

Fear now began to turn to dread as he anticipated the hardships he would face. Matt put his head down and began to drag his feet as he continued to walk towards the mountain. After a couple minutes, he heard someone say something to him. A tall, well built man was walking in the opposite direction as him. He had a large coil of rope over his shoulder, a hiking backpack on, climbing carabineers visible filling a small pouch on his waist, and he was sporting some new hiking boots. The man also seemed to be decked from head to foot in North Face apparel.

"You headed toward the mountain?" the man asked.

"Yeah," Matt replied reluctantly, "that's where I'm headed."

The man tightened his neck and pulled his head back as if shocked by Matt's response. "Um, where is all your gear? That is a pretty steep mountain, and it can get pretty cold at night. You are wearing shorts and tennis shoes!"

Matt glanced down at his clothes. He truly wasn't prepared for the weather on the mountain. As he glanced up towards the mountain, he now saw that snow blanketed the top of it. Matt's eyes returned to the man who was still staring at him with a puzzled look.

"Well?" the man asked as his eye brows raised. Having no response Matt just shrugged his shoulders. The man shook his head and began to walk off mumbling to himself as he was leaving. The last audible thing Matt heard was something about how foolish he thought Matt was for not being prepared.

After hearing that Matt's attitude became a lot more gloomy. His head returned to staring at the ground while he walked. His hands no longer hung at his sides gliding through the grass. Both hands now rested deep within his pockets.

"I didn't even know I was going to have to climb a mountain. I couldn't have been prepared." Matt said out loud to himself.

Looking up, Matt saw a similar bearded, dark haired, tan skin man walking towards him. Matt quickly realized that it was once again Jesus. He smiled as he came alongside Matt and said, "How's it going?"

Matt, not really being in the conversational mood, just nodded his head in a motion signaling Jesus to look towards the mountain ahead of him. He glanced toward it and said, "Yeah?"

Matt shook his head and said, "I'm not prepared to climb the mountain and don't know what to do. I feel a little foolish for not being prepared."

"Well," Jesus replied slowly as if giving Matt's statement some deep thought, "did you know you were going to be headed there?"

"No, not really," Matt said back.

"How could you have been more prepared then?" Jesus asked.

Matt didn't look at Jesus when he answered, he just returned his eyes to the grass at his feet. "I want to be prepared for everything. It kind of feels like I failed in not being prepared even if I didn't know I would need all that stuff."

They continued walking for a short distance without Jesus responding. Matt was just beginning to realize how tired he was from walking when the ground began to slant downward. Noticing this, his head jerked up, and he saw that he was indeed now walking down a small hill. For some reason this ravine had not been visible the whole time Matt had been walking through the field. At the bottom of the hill was a small stream. The hill slanting up on the other side of the steam was much steeper than the one they were currently walking down. Across the stream, built into the side of the hill, was a Starbucks with a wooded deck in front. The deck actually looked more like a dock than a deck. It had tall posts that kept it far above the stream.

Matt glanced over at Jesus and saw that he had a smile stretched across his face. They both hopped across the stream and climbed half way up the other side until they could pull themselves onto the deck. They both took a seat at one of the tables. Conveniently, there were even a couple drinks there for them.

After taking a few sips, Jesus began talking again. "So what are you so worried about?"

"I don't feel prepared for the task before me. How am I going to get over the mountain?" Matt responded.

Jesus' brows drew together as he replied, "It is a long way off still. You don't need to worry about that. I will provide what you need when you need it."

"Yeah, but I feel like I should prepare the best I can. I don't want to waste my time or act foolishly like the climber said I was." Matt responded.

"Well what have you come up with so far?"

Matt looked back at Jesus and slowly dragged out, "nothing."

Jesus asked Matt, "What does my word say to do?"

"Not to worry," Matt asserted, "but knowing I shouldn't worry doesn't make it any easier not to!"

After taking a few more sips while looking into Matt's eyes, Jesus calmly responded, "So for a considerable amount of time now, you have been worrying about how to get over the mountain in your path. You realized that worrying about it or trying to plan is not going to get you any closer to being more prepared. However, you continue to dwell on the possible problems that you might face. You do this even though you know I promise to provide and watch over you. If you were going to go over the mountain I would provide all that you need to do it, but did you ever consider that you might not even be going over it?"

Matt just sat there staring at his drink. His fingers spun the cup around and around as he fidgeted with it. "Where else would I be heading?" he finally responded.

"Just trust me." Jesus answered with a small smile forming. "Trust me and don't dwell on assumptions and worries."

Just then, Matt heard a noise in the distance. The noise was slowly growing louder and louder. He thought it almost sounded like a rushing river. He eyes kept steady in the direction from which the sound came. Suddenly, a huge wave appeared from behind a bend in the ravine. A wall of water quickly rushed towards them. In what felt like a few seconds, the wall of water passed by them just as quickly as it had appeared. Matt's eyes followed the surge of water. The water showed no sign of relenting. The small stream had now become a decent size river.

Once again Matt heard a sound from around the bend in the ravine. This time it sounded like a dull humming of a motor. Sure enough, a small boat came around the bend headed their way.

Matt's eyes glanced back at Jesus and noticed his smile had significantly grown. "You aren't going to the mountain Matt. There is a pass over yonder," as he signaled with his hand toward the direction the water was flowing. "I knew all along I would provide this river and boat to carry you through. There is no way you could have known, but that is why you have to trust Me. My ways are not your ways. Until you truly believe that I provide, lead, and protect, you will never worry any less."

Matt felt a little foolish for his folly of worrying and had no response. He just sat there gripping his cup with both hands and looking over at Jesus. Jesus continued to smile and said, "You better go catch your boat."

Matt awoke once again to the rote noise of Michele's alarm. He went through the motions of preparing breakfast and the coffee. Matt ate his breakfast slowly with his arm draped around Michele's shoulder. When she left for work she kissed him goodbye and said, "We'll be alright. God will provide." Her last statement slid into a warm smile as she headed out the door.

Matt now sat down on the couch pondering what to do with his day. Before, one of the things that got him through the day was knowing that his lay off was temporary. Now he wondered how it would even be possible not to meditate on feelings of worthlessness all day. After staring out the window for ten minutes, he reached over and grabbed his Bible from the coffee table. Not knowing where to read he just started in Genesis.

Hour after hour he read. He saw how God always followed through with his promises. He saved Noah and his family, provided a son for Abraham and Sarah, greatly multiplied Jacob's family, and He always provided what they needed.

As Matt finished up reading Genesis, he realized it was well past his normal lunch time. He made a sandwich and went back to the living room to continue reading. Exodus amazed Matt reading how God provided. All of the Israelites wandered around in the desert without food. God sent food in the same way He now sends dew in the mornings. Bread flakes called manna would appear every morning, and God also directed flocks of quail to their camps. Matt had known this story from childhood, but he had not remembered that God only provided one day at a time. If someone tried to store enough manna for two days it would waste away and rot.

Matt began to realize how much he and Michele still had even though he had lost his job. Michele still had her job, and they had emergency funds in the bank saved for times like this. "God will provide what I need when I need it," Matt said to himself. After he said that, he remembered all the feelings from the day before of feeling the responsibility of not being able to provide for Michele now. "God if you command me to lead my wife and instill in me the instinct to provide for her, why would you put me in a position where I can't do that?"

He felt the Holy Spirit answering him with, "You are to be the spiritual leader. I want you to lead your wife to grow closer to Me through this time. I am responsible for providing for you both, and I will. It is your responsibility to seek Me and get to know Me. I will lead you. You are currently looking at the mountain ahead of you. I will either provide the gear to make the trek or the river to avoid the mountain. Rest in me."

Matt began to understand that God had put him in this position so that he would learn to trust Him. However, knowing that didn't make it any easier to trust God.

After he had read in Genesis and Exodus, Matt spent the rest of the day cleaning the house and getting dinner ready. Even though he was busy with the household chores, his thoughts stayed consumed with worries. After awhile his worries turned into fears. What if we can't pay our bills? What if we lose our house? Thoughts like these began to run wild in his mind, and he could feel himself getting more tense. In an attempt to forget everything going on, Matt just turned on the radio to try to drown them out with music.

The following day Matt woke up still troubled by the same worries and fears. After Michele left for work, Matt began reading in Exodus where he had left off the day before. Once again he was amazed with the manna God continued to provide. Matt had stopped reading mid chapter yesterday, and finishing that chapter today left him with another thought to ponder. God provided manna for the entire forty years that the Israelites lived in the wilderness. For forty years they would go to bed at night knowing that if God did not provide manna the next day then they would have nothing to eat. They were put into a position where they had no option but to trust God.

As a kid in Sunday school, he had heard the stories about Israel, but they seemed different than the story he was now reading. Before, they seemed so foolish for not trusting God at His word, and it was very easy for Matt to criticize them for it. Yet now, he could finally understand them better because he was put into a position of having to trust God to provide. Even though Matt had only read half a chapter today, he decided to just think of what God had said to him through that passage.

Being a nice day out, Matt decided to work on the patio in the back yard. While he worked he kept praying about what God had shown him that morning. After awhile he even began to pray aloud. "Lord, I want to learn to trust you, yet it is an incredibly hard thing to do. I've been taught that I just need to try harder when times get tough. It seems your Word on the other hand is just telling me to trust You will provide. How can I not constantly think about the problem of not having a job?"

As he was praying, Matt saw his neighbor Harold headed towards him. After a couple minutes of small talk, Harold asked if Matt could take him to the grocery store to buy some groceries. Matt said he would be glad to, but he inquired why he needed a ride. His neighbor told him that his truck had some engine problems that needed fixed; and because he only got a small amount each month from his retirement plan, he would have to save up a while to fix it. Matt enjoyed the opportunity to spend some time with him and felt good about helping him out.

When they arrived home from the store, Matt returned to working on the patio. He had only been working a couple minutes when he felt the Holy Spirit saying to him, "I want you to give Harold the money to fix his truck."

Matt's first emotion was fear. Why would God tell him to do something like that at a time like this? Matt was already worried that he would run out of money. Would God really ask him to give away money when he had no job? Excuse after excuse popped into Matt's mind. He wasn't even sure how he and Michele were going to make it. "I don't even know how we will pay our bills God. I can't do that. If we had more of a safety net, and I still had a job I could give him the money."

The rest of the day was spent trying to forget what the Holy Spirit had put on his heart. Matt wanted to pray, but every time he tried talking to God his thoughts went straight to helping Harold. Matt began to get frustrated that God wouldn't say anything to him besides that. That evening it was difficult for him to fall asleep because of those thoughts.

The following morning Matt realized that sleeping on it did not help him forget what the Lord had put on his heart the previous day. After Michele left for work, Matt went straight to work on the patio again. He knew if he opened up his Bible God would once again just say that He wanted him to help Harold. "I can't do it," he kept repeating to himself. "Giving money away is not an option right now." Hardening his heart and mind, Matt began to push the voice telling him to give out of his head. "I won't think about it anymore," he told himself.

The rest of the day Matt's frustration grew. His worries and fears began to turn more into an anger and bitterness. 'God if you love me so much why would You let me lose my job?' he kept thinking. His mood steadily declined throughout the day as well. By the afternoon he had begun feeling that it was his inadequacy that had lost him his job. When evening came, he was once again feeling depressed. As Matt struggled to fall asleep that evening, he began negative self talk: 'It is your fault you lost your job. Your wife is providing for you now, and you are less of a man. She will start to lose respect for you if you don't provide for her needs.'

On Friday Matt and I met once again. This time however, Matt was not a half an hour early; he was actually five minutes late. His frustrated mood was visible from his face the minute he sat down. Before he had been pliable and desiring to change, yet that day he came seemingly just to vent. He told me about how he kept having notions that he should give his neighbor money to fix his truck. He elaborated all the reasons he felt he couldn't do it. "It is simply not an option. We don't have the money, but I can't get it off my mind!"

I began to ask Matt what God had been teaching him that week. Matt's demeanor slowly began to change from that point on. He told me about God teaching him about trust and how hard it had been for him. Matt also admitted that he didn't really want to learn to trust God; he desired much more for God just to provide for him in a different way. "For example if I had a job," Matt began, "then I would be able to rest in God. I would see that He is providing for me and would be able to praise Him for it. Not having a job just causes me stress."

"How often did you thank God for your job while you had it?" I interjected.

This question caused Matt to smile shyly and reply, "Good point."

I asked Matt to elaborate more on how the issue of helping his neighbor first came up. Though he tightened back up a little when I asked, he still responded calmly. "I had been praying for the Lord to teach me how to trust Him. My neighbor came over asking for a ride; I took him; and when we arrived home it just popped into my mind."

I followed up his reply with the question, "Do you think it was the Holy Spirit who put it on your heart?"

"I did at first," he said, "but now that I just worry about it I feel like it is just my mind not letting it go. I know I need to let it go though because it isn't an option."

"Does it come back into your mind when you pray?" I asked.

His eyes looked up towards the ceiling as if in thought and he responded, "Yeah, pretty much every time. Every time I have tried reading my Bible since then it has come up too. I don't even have to read anything. I just open my Bible and am immediately bombarded by those thoughts."

I nodded to acknowledge what he said and replied, "I am not you and thus cannot get into your brain. What I am about to say is something for you to think about. I am not saying that it is positively true for you, but I am going to give you my opinion. Whenever the Holy Spirit convicts me of something, He will put in on my mind constantly. I have a pretty domineering conscience, and it is impossible for me to forget anything He has put on my heart to do. How I verify that it is God speaking into my life and not just random thoughts is through prayer and reading His word. The fact that the idea of giving to your neighbor comes up while you are praying and reading your Bible indicates that it is very likely God putting it on your heart. Do you think it's possible that this is Him giving you an opportunity to trust Him fully?"

Matt scrunched his eyebrows at this and asked what I meant. "Well," I continued, "Not having a job puts you in the position of having to trust God to provide. You had tried to find another job the whole time that you were partially employed and had not found one. Thus you had no choice to be in your current situation. However, if you were to give that money to your neighbor, you would be willingly putting your care and your needs in His hands. It is, in effect, an outward action to show that you trust God will provide for you. By giving money away when you need it most, you will be showing that your security is not found in your money but in God."

Matt took a slow drink of water from the bottle he had brought that morning. He slowly exhaled with his lips closed pushing his cheeks out. "That makes sense," he finally said after a long pause.

Deciding to tackle a different issue, I then asked him how he had felt while trying to push it all out of his head the last couple days. "Terrible. I began to get mad at my current situation and at God. My anger turned into depression, and I started feeling worthless again."

"Matt," I began again, "you feeling that way, to me, just verifies that it truly is God's voice in your life right now. You have been praying that you want to grow closer to God, and He has now presented you with an opportunity to do so. However, when we as believers do not listen to what the Holy Spirit puts on our heart then we are bound to feel miserable. In your case, it seems you know God is telling you to trust Him and give your neighbor the money, but it is so hard for you to do that you would rather try to convince yourself it wasn't God who told you to do it.

"One of the key verses that comes up in almost everyone of my counseling sessions is I Timothy 1:19. It basically says, 'Keeping faith and a good conscience, which some have rejected and suffered shipwreck in regards to their faith.' This verse emphasizes the importance of a good conscience. When you are convicted of something by God or He places something on your heart to do, then not doing it will dirty your conscience. That is why you couldn't get it off your mind and you felt so guilty about it. The Holy Spirit talks to us when we listen. If you were to harden your heart and refuse to listen to God on this issue at hand, then very shortly you will stop hearing Him speak into your life. Following closely behind that is the depression you know all too well.

"One thing I feel most Christians don't understand is that not listening to God in the little things is what leads to many mental disturbances like depression. Everyone wants to argue that it isn't a sin issue because they aren't out committing 'big' sins like adultery or murder, yet being unwilling to submit to God's commands on a daily basis is bound to cause some hardships because believers know better."

Not much else was said during our session that day. Matt seemed to have a lot on his mind already and now had plenty of new things to mull over. When Michele got home that evening, Matt told her all about giving to Harold. He told her how God had put it on his heart, what God had been teaching him about trust that week, how he had fought it the last couple days, and about our conversation. When she asked him what he thought about it now, he replied, "I feel like we should do it. If we say we believe God will provide for us, then we should put our money where our mouth is."

After dinner Matt and Michele headed over to Harold's house. While handing him the check for the two hundred fifty dollars, Matt gave a quick explanation. "God has continually provided for our needs and will continue to. Michele and I feel that God wants to use us to provide for you today. So here you go!"

Harold was a little surprised but very grateful. Walking back to their house hand in hand, Matt realized that his heart was once again at peace. Willingly putting himself in the hands of God's provision definitely felt more comforting than striving to provide by himself and tightly holding on to what he had.

CHAPTER SIX

That weekend Matt and Michele had gone through all their finances and made a plan for the next several months. On Monday, Matt began submitting resumes several places around town. Tuesday and Wednesday he also went job searching. By Thursday Matt was once again feeling significant weight on his shoulders for not having a job. He was even looking at a variety of jobs that he would have never before considered, but he felt desperate for any job. Everywhere he went it seemed no one was hiring. Frustration began to set in by Wednesday not yet having found a single possible job opening. Thursday he began to seriously stress out. 'What if I can't find a job for months?' he thought to himself. He began to relook over all his and Michele's finances even though they had already done that. Something in him felt the need to do it again in hopes of finding some security it knowing they had enough for several months.

As he was doing that, he realized he had already lost track of what he learned the week before. Once again he was putting his confidence in his savings account instead of trusting in God. Realizing this frustrated him. "I just learned last week the importance of trusting God whole heartily," he began saying to himself, "and less than a week later I am acting like I totally forgot! I wish I would just learn to continually trust God and walk with Him."

What frustrated Matt the most was that he didn't want to worry. He would constantly think of all the reasons he should not worry, but no matter how hard he tried he constantly began to worry again. After he had once again looked through all their finances, he now felt less secure than he did before. "I have to figure out how to not worry," he said out loud while thinking, "God commands me not to worry. I have to try harder to quit."

Matt put away all the financial records and got out his Bible. He had finished Exodus earlier in the week and was most of the way through Leviticus now. However, all the laws seemed to be mundane to him, so he decided to read in the New Testament today. Skimming through the books, he decided to read Romans. He read the whole book in about an hour but didn't feel like he got very much out of it. It all seemed a little too lofty and theological for him. The only thing he felt he understood was in Romans chapter seven. 'Paul also did things he doesn't want to do, like me worrying when I want so badly not to,' he thought.

"God," he began praying, "I am sorry for worrying and getting frustrated this week about a job. I know You command me not to worry and to break any of Your commands is sin. I know I should trust You. It is not only the trust issue either. No matter what I struggle with in my life I never seem to be able to master it. Lord why can't I just do what you command? I try so hard and yet always fail. Why is it so difficult to abstain from sin?" With that he laid down and slowly drifted into sleep.

Matt was now sitting in a damp, dark cave. He was perched on an oval stone which was about a foot and a half tall. The stone lay near the mouth of the cave which opened into a desert. Dark clouds loomed in the night sky covering moon and stars alike, and even the desert appeared deserted and black. The only sound Matt could hear was the crackling fire which was a couple feet in front of him. On the other side of the fire, he saw a man scrunched down in a squatting position. His knees where at his chest and his arms wrapped around his legs. Matt could see that the man was looking at him, but since the fire put out minimal light and an overabundance of smoke it was difficult to get a very close look at his facial features.

"Hello son," the man said to Matt.

Matt, now confused, scratched his head and cynically replied, "Do I know you?"

"Well," the man began again, "sort of but not really. I'm Adam. You know, the first human being?"

"Oh." Matt said as a smile curled up on his face. "That would be why you called me your son. Makes sense I guess."

Adam smiled back and said, "Yup!"

"Well, where is Eve then?" Matt asked.

"She is in the back of our home sleeping."

"So this is your home hmm?" Matt asked but quickly added with a smirk, "love what you have done with the place." Adam smiled and let out a little laugh.

Adam then stood from his crouching position. He was a tall, slender, yet muscular man. Matt smiled to himself when he saw Adam was wearing a primitive loin cloth. He wanted to make a joke about being glad he met Adam after the fall so he wouldn't be naked, but he refrained because he didn't think making a joke about mankind's first sin was very appropriate. Adam walked over and sat down on a large stone closer to Matt. He tossed a couple more logs on the fire which made the flames light up the cave much more.

"I guess we have some things to talk about," Adam began. "I hear you want to know why it is so difficult for you not to sin and why no matter how hard you strive you always fail and end up sinning again."

"You know?" Matt asked with an air of surprise written on his face. "Yeah, that would be awesome if you could tell me that!"

"I doubt you will say it's awesome after I tell you," Adam explained, "because it isn't really the best news for you."

At this Matt's face contorted a little and now sported a very puzzled look. Adam then continued on, "It is going to take a bit of explaining. If you get confused at all, just stop me and ask a question." Adam put his hands together and rubbed them as he started the explanation, "Let's start at the beginning. God created the world and created me as the head of the human race. I represented the entire human race. Therefore what was true for me was true of the rest of the human race coming after me. Lucky I am so good looking right?" He paused for a second with a big smile while glancing over at Matt for assurance that his joke was funny.

After a short pause, his smile slid flat on his face and he let out a long sigh before he continued talking. "And well, you see, um, I kind of screwed up really big as you know. But the consequences for my actions didn't just affect me. They were credited or transferred down to those who came after me, to all those who came after me in my likeness. This means that the rest of the human race all received the complete consequences of my actions because you are all identified with me."

Matt stopped him here for a second by raising his hand slightly to imply he needed a moment to process. "So what you are saying is that because you sinned, I get the consequences for your sin?" Matt said with a slightly confused look still on his face.

Adam continued on, "Yes, unfortunately for you it is true. Let's take a look at a verse from Romans. 'Through the one man's disobedience the many were made sinners.'[1] What this says is, that through my one sin, all mankind became sinners."

"So I am a sinner because of you?" Matt clarified.

Adam slowly nodded his head in agreement. "Matt most people in your day don't understand the gravity of their sin. Most believe they are sinners because they sin, but the truth is that they sin because they are sinners. My sin was passed on to them and they were born sinners."

"Yeah, I still don't completely follow what the significance of this is. I know I am a sinner," Matt replied.

Adam tilted his head to the side, and Matt could see his eyes look up and to the right as if he was thinking very intently. Then with an "Aha!" and a raise of his finger, Adam began again, "I have an illustration for you. You bear the last name of your parents. You did nothing to be born into the family you are in and can do nothing to change who your parents are. The only way you can get out of your family is death. You are a member of that family and have the family name and get the family inheritance."

"Okay," Matt said, "but what is the significance of it?"

"In the same way as being born into your family, you were born into my family. You bear my name which happens to be called sinful flesh, and you also inherited my punishment which is death. Just like Romans says, 'Just as through one man sin entered into the world, and death through sin, and so death spread to all men, because all sinned.[2]'"

"I understand that now. I know that all humans are going to die because of sin, but I don't feel you are answering the initial question. Why can't I stop sinning and why do I do things that I know I shouldn't do?" Matt asked.

"I'm almost there," Adam said. "The death you inherited from me is much more than the physical death of your body. This death is separation from God. Through this death you were condemned to be separated from God for your entire life unable to fellowship with Him; and then after death you were to be eternally separated from God in hell. In Romans, Paul uses the word condemnation to describe this death. You are condemned to this death, and this death rules over all your experiences in life. The inheritance you got from me is slavery to sin and death."

Now this got Matt's mind turning. He had never thought of himself as a slave to sin, because it was always a choice he made to sin. His conception of a slave is someone in chains getting dragged where they didn't want to go. As Matt pondered the concept for a minute, he tried to formulate his thoughts into a question. Finally, after several minutes of silence he asked, "How can I be a slave to sin if I am the one who chooses to sin? Slaves don't have the privilege of choices."

"Well to use another analogy, think of your body as a factory, and that factory produces sin and sin alone. The characteristics of the sinful flesh which you inherited from me are adultery, fornication, uncleanness, idolatry, hatred, strife, jealousy, wrath, envying, murder, drunkenness, and similar things. Your flesh can produce some 'positive' characteristics of love, joy, peace, longsuffering, and gentleness, however even these are facsimiles and useless. All the characteristics of the flesh, negative or those that appear positive, are unacceptable to God because of the source of all these characteristics. All of these characteristics and actions come from self. All come from the condemned life you have because of your relation to me. Even Paul understood this when he stated, 'For I know that nothing good dwells in me, that is, my flesh.'[3] In the flesh, you can do nothing good for God in this life."

Matt again slightly raised his hand as if to request silence. He began to think over what had just been said. Even his good deeds were not pleasing to God. It did not even seem possible! How could it not please God when he did something nice for another person? That is what he had been taught to do his whole life! "I don't know if I believe that," Matt finally said.

Adam exhaled slowly and nodded his head as if to acknowledge Matt's internal struggle. "I am going to have to leave you with this;" Adam began, "You were born a slave to sin. From then on sin ruled every aspect of who you are. Sin is what you desire and what you do. You were born inheriting my penalty, which in a sense you could say you were born 'in Adam.' That means all that was mine is now yours. You were born into slavery to sin and death, and the only way out of my family is death."

"What does it all mean then? Am I doomed to just go on sinning till I die?" Matt shot back quickly, "You have to tell me how I can quit sinning and please God!"

Adam just shook his head and replied, "That is not my place to do. I am just here to lay the ground work and explain where you came from."

And with that Adam was gone. It appeared to Matt that in a poof he just disappeared. Once the conversation had ended, Matt realized how hard the stone was that he had been sitting on. He stood up and decided to walk towards the mouth of the cave. As he walked closer and closer to the cave's mouth, it began to get more and more light out. As he was about to exit the cave, it was so bright that he had to close his eyes.

Matt's eyes strained under the brightness that now surrounded him. Slowly his eyes began to hurt less, and he could tell it was no longer so bright around him. When he opened them, the cave and desert were gone. He now stood facing the cross. Actually, all three crosses were in front of him. He was on top of a very rocky hill, and as he glanced over his shoulder, he noticed behind him lay Jerusalem.

Looking back towards the cross, he now found Jesus standing at his side. "Why am I here?" Matt asked with the look of a child asking a question to his parent.

Jesus glanced over at Matt and asked, "What is the significance of the cross?"

Matt, putting forth all his effort not to misspeak, began his explanation. "After You lived Your sinless life here on earth, You were crucified for the sins of the world. On the cross all of the sin of the world fell upon You, and God the Father poured out His wrath on that sin. You died as a holy sacrifice so that we would not have to pay the penalty for our own sin. Three days later You rose from the dead proving that death had no power over You. The significance of this is that all who believe on You as their savior will be saved from the punishment of their sin. We are saved by faith apart from any works, and through belief we will no longer be destined for hell."

Jesus nodded his head in agreement and replied, "What else?"

After a short pause, Matt just repeated, "What else?" with a confused inflection.

"Yeah," Jesus answered. "What else is significant about the cross? All you told me about was how the cross is important to keep you from hell after you physically die. What is the significance of it here on earth?"

Matt just stared at Jesus with a dumbfounded look. He couldn't think of what Jesus was getting at because Matt had always been taught that his explanation was the full extent of the work of the cross. Shrugging his shoulders, he admitted that he didn't know.

Jesus once again nodded his head in acknowledgement before he began talking. "You are definitely not alone in that Matt. A large number of my children don't know that the cross is significant in your daily life. Too many of My children think they were saved from the penalty of sin, hell, and left on earth to be stricken full of guilt and to realize the impossibility for them to ever stop sinning. To them the Holy Spirit seems to only be a constant conviction of the sin in their lives. They believe the Bible gives an impossible command to be holy,[4] and then they were left on earth just to realize that they cannot."

"Jesus?" Matt interrupted. Jesus paused from his talking and waited for Matt to continue. As Matt continued, the earnestness of what he said could easily be read on his face. "Adam told me that I was born a slave to sin. He said that I was doomed to live in sin and that even my good deeds aren't pleasing to You. If what he said was true, then aren't we believers given the impossible task to be holy?"

"That is actually what the masses are uniformed about!" Jesus passionately responded. "The reason you cannot produce the righteousness My Father demands is because of your position in relation to Adam. In Adam, all are condemned and cannot please My Father. That is why I had to be born of a virgin, so I would not be born into Adam's line."

Matt and Jesus both sat down on a couple large stones facing the crosses. As Matt observed the cross, Jesus continued talking. "This is where the significance of the cross comes into play for you as My child. When you first believed all that you stated earlier about the significance of the cross, you became My child. You were then baptized with the Holy Spirit who began to reside in you from that point on. The beauty of that is shown in Romans: 'Or do you not know that all of us who have been baptized into Christ Jesus have been baptized into His death.'[5] Adam told you the truth when he said you had to die to be freed from his family and slavery to sin, but when you were baptized by the Holy Spirit you were baptized into My death."

Matt felt a little confused and repeated the phrase "baptized into his death" as he continued to listen to Jesus.

"This means that you did die and were removed from your family and position 'in Adam'. Once again just as it says in Romans, 'The free gift is not like the transgression. For if by the transgression of the one the many died, much more did the grace of God and the gift by the grace of the one Man, Jesus Christ, abound to the many. The gift is not like that which came through the one who sinned; for on the one hand the judgment arose from the one transgression resulting in condemnation, but on the other hand the free gift arose from many transgressions resulting in justification.'[6] Just as through Adam's one transgression, aka his sin, he passed on his sinful flesh and condemnation to you, but through my many transgressions, aka my sinless life and death, I passed on justification and reconciliation to you."

Matt had heard the word reconciliation used before but definitely didn't grasp the gravity of the word. Understanding this, Jesus elaborated a little more.

"Reconciliation carries with it a sense of being restored. It means that once believing on my death and resurrection you are restored to a relationship with Me and My Father. You are restored to the eternal life that Adam had before his sin!"

This statement confused Matt. How could he have that perfect unbroken relationship with God since he was a sinner? Adam had that beautiful relationship only before he sinned. Matt understood that God removed Adam from the garden because he would continue to sin and because he was now condemned to death. So how could Matt now have that same relationship with God when He knew he would continue to sin?

Jesus began to answer Matt's thoughts. "Remember when we had our chat in the jungle? I told you how you were now accepted by My Father based on my righteousness. Look at yourself Matt." Looking down Matt saw himself covered in dirt, grease, slime, everything gross you can think of. Matt realized that this was all of his sin. Jesus then wrapped a huge white sheet all around him that said 'In Christ' on it.

"From the moment you believed on Me, you became part of My family. In My family, just as in Adam's family, you inherit the family name and inheritance. You now hold the title of child of God," Christ told him, "And My Father chose before the foundation of the world, that He would view all those who belong to Me by My righteousness instead of your sin. When He now looks at you He sees this perfect white sheet which is My righteousness. He now accepts you as holy because I am holy."

This sent a joyful thrill down Matt's body. "God sees me as holy now?" he asked.

"He sees My holiness in you because you are My child. Therefore in the same way you inherited Adam's sin you inherited My righteousness. You are now restored to a relationship with My Father based on My righteousness not your own. That is how you can be reconciled once again to that perfect relationship."

"Wow," was all Matt could say. He sat there staring at the cross thinking of the magnitude of God's grace to him. He also thought of the pressure this removed from his shoulders to try to act perfect and sinless all the time. All his life after becoming a believer he had felt the pressure of trying to make himself more pleasing to God. When he thought of that he remembered his sin and struggles to quit sinning. "What about all my sin, Jesus? I still sin. Does God just overlook it all because He knows that I will continue to sin here on earth?"

"Well, there is more the cross did for you besides all we have just talked about," Jesus answered. "Not only did I take away your penalty for sin and restore you to a relationship with Me, I also took away the power of sin in your life. Not only did I die that day on the cross, your flesh and sin nature died there with Me. Once again Romans clearly states this in saying: 'Knowing this, that our old self was crucified with Him, in order that our body of sin might be done away with, so that we would no longer be slaves to sin.'[7]

"This verse states the fact that you inherited my death. Remember how Adam told you the only way out of his family was death? That is why this death you inherited from Me is so important. It was the only way you could be removed from your family 'in Adam' and be put into My family 'in Christ!' The significance of this also means that you are dead to that part of your old life. You are no longer a slave to sin like you once were."

Matt shifted on the stone as Jesus was talking. It was difficult for him to take it all in. How could he be completely free from sin yet still do it when he didn't want to? Jesus smiled before continuing, "You not only inherited My death, you also inherited My burial and resurrection! Once again Romans clearly says, 'Therefore we have been buried with Him through baptism into death.'[8] This burial is proof of your death with Me for only dead people are buried; and just as certain as your death and burial with Me is your resurrection with Me![9] The death and resurrection that you inherited together become life changing. The death of your sinful flesh through crucifixion only separated you from your slavery to sin.[10] But much more than that, just as I was, My children were resurrected from the dead that they too might now walk in the same newness of life.[11]

"What this means is that not only were you separated from your old self in Adam, you are joined to your new self in Me. Your condemnation was taken away and replaced with life. Not just any life, you were given My life. My life lives in you!"

Matt's face was now vividly expressing his confusion. Jesus noticed his expression and suggested they go for a walk. For the first few minutes of their walk not much was said. Matt was still trying to process all he had heard. After the long silence, Jesus finally began talking again. "I know it is really hard to grasp the significance of all this, but it is life changing news. Let's go back to why Adam and I told you the things we did. You were struggling with the fact that you sin even when you try hard not to. The Bible commanded you not to worry, you tried really hard not to worry, and the next thing you know you had been compulsively worrying for two days straight. I allowed you to talk to Adam to see where you came from, your roots, so to speak. Then I wanted to show you who you now are. I told you how you were now accepted by My Father based on My righteousness and not your own. My Father now looks at you and sees My righteousness and therefore accepts you as holy. He sees My righteousness in you because My life has resided in you ever since you were baptized by the Spirit!

"All this to say that when you strive to do good and attempt to think of as many ways as possible to stop your sin habits, you are going back to your old roots in Adam. Even when you strive to do good, it is tainted by the sin of self. All man's strivings are as worthless rags to My Father and cannot please Him. Through death with Me on the cross, you have freedom from all sin. If you give into sin, you are returning to your old master and willingly making yourself its slave."

Matt nodded a little to show that he was now tracking with Jesus, but at the same time he still struggled a little with the concepts. One thing in particular now seemed extremely unknown to him. After formulating it into a question, he asked, "So how is it possible to please God then?"

Jesus' response seemed too simple to be true. "Matt, I desire that you get to know My Father and Me. When you read My Word and talk to Me on a regular basis, you will get to know Me better. As you get to know Me better, more of My life will begin to be revealed in you. As you understand My character of love, you will begin to love as I do. As you begin to understand My inability to break a promise, you will learn to trust Me more. Since I already reside in you, when you seek to know Me more and more, everyone else will begin to see My life being lived through you. If you strive to do good deeds in attempt to please My Father and make yourself more pleasing to Him, then you are toiling in vain. I am completely satisfying to Him, and I reside in you. When He looks at you He sees me. As you get to know Me and follow Me closely, others will also begin to see My life being lived through you. How you please Me is by seeking to know Me more. The rest will be done through you."

VERSE REFRENCES

1) Romans 5:19a
2) Romans 5:12
3) Romans 7:18a
4) I Peter 1:16
5) Romans 6:3
6) Romans 5:15-16
7) Romans 6:6
8) Romans 6:4a
9) Romans 6:5
10) Romans 6:6
11) Romans 6:4

CHAPTER SEVEN

Monday of the following week Matt was back to his routine of being a half an hour early for his appointments. I pride myself in being able to notice body language and facial cues on people, but I am pretty sure anyone could have figured out Matt's mood by his face, posture, and demeanor. On this day he seemed very composed. He was calm, his thoughts were collected, and he spoke more slowly than he had at other times. His frantic frustration from the week before was now thankfully gone, and I sensed he was for some reason strangely comfortable with his current position of being jobless.

Matt came in and took a seat at his usual place. I followed him over to the side of the room and also took a seat. "So how have you been Matt?" I asked.

Matt folded his upper lip into his mouth, and his eyes glanced up towards the ceiling. Seeing that he was considering his answer, I just waited. After about fifteen seconds he replied, "It's going well. Actually," pausing once again for a few seconds, "It has been hard, really hard. But I am learning things. God is showing me how to walk more closely with Him, and though it is hard, I know it's good."

After he finished talking, he just let out a small sigh and a gentle smile slid onto his face.

I asked him to elaborate, and he went into a lot of detail about the previous week. He told me about the frustration he felt and the worrying that took place. He told me how many places he had applied, all the places he had called, and how fruitless the job search had been so far. Matt then explained how his worrying had grown as the week had dragged on.

Shifting from talking about his emotions and the job search, he told me about his dreams. As he went into detail explaining the truth God had revealed to him, I began to grow more and more amazed at its depth. It fascinated me how Jesus quoted Romans and basically explained to Matt what he had read. What was really cool is that I even learned several things while he explained it all.

Once he had finished telling me about his week up to that point and giving a thorough retelling of his dream, I asked him what he has learned since then. "Well," he began, "Things have been going well but at the same time are very difficult. I woke up from my dream excited about what Jesus had taught me. I was amazed by how much more I learned about God's acceptance of me. My previous dream in the jungle with Jesus had comforted me quite a bit, but I learned about it much more in depth this time. It changes my understanding of God's dealings with me significantly knowing that He views me based on Christ's righteousness instead of my sin.

"All of a sudden I realized I don't have worry, nor should I worry, about whether God is mad or upset with me. He knows I am going to sin, but by His grace He allows me to still come before Him and talk with Him. His relationship with Me is based on Christ's righteousness, not mine. This is so huge for me!" Matt passionately exclaimed. "Because for years whenever I would sin or do something I know God commands I shouldn't, I would feel dejected. I felt as if I was constantly on a holiness ladder. Whenever I sinned I would take a step down, and if I sinned a lot I would move down the ladder a ton. Whenever I did something good, in my mind I moved up the ladder a step or two. That was how I rated if God was pleased with me or not. When I sinned lots it felt like there was no way God would listen to me after all I had done, but I now realize that none of that is true. There is no holiness ladder. God views people two ways: in Adam or in Christ. He views man either by man's sinfulness or He views them by Christ's righteousness. And since I am a child of God, I am now accepted in His sight.

"Not only was I excited about all that, I also began to understand what it means to have the life of Christ living inside of me. Paul's words 'For me to live is Christ'[1] finally makes sense to me. Christ's righteousness, that God now sees when He looks at me, resides inside of me. I know it doesn't mean I will completely stop sinning now that I know that, but it will change how I will live. Instead of trying to force myself to do things God commands, I now see that in those moments I need to turn to Him.

"The last couple days whenever I began to worry I would pray, 'God I am starting to worry again. This is so hard to trust that You are in control when nothing seems to be happening and I still have no leads for a job. Please give me comfort, peace, and the wisdom to know what to do.' The first time I prayed that I, sat on my couch and asked, 'What do you want me to do?' As I sat there quietly he brought verse after verse to mind. Verses like 'come to Me and you will find rest for your soul'[2] and 'do not worry about your life for God sustains the lilies and the grass will he not do the same for His children'.[3]

"In that moment, I began to have peace come over me and I felt the Lord tell me, 'I want you to go write a note to Michele and put it in her Bible. Remind her how much you love her, and that you know God will provide for you both.' I was even more comforted after I did that, but it didn't stop there. I realized what it meant to have the life of Christ in me. Even if I had tried my very best to stop worrying, all I would have done is made myself busy all day and a little frustrated because I still would have the worry in the back of my mind. But by turning to God in the hard moment, I had a peace that definitely didn't come from me. Also, God reached out and used me to encourage my wife. Christ performed an action of love through me to my wife. I finally understood that listening to and obeying God in the little daily things is how Christ lives His life through us."

Once he finished speaking, I must have looked a little overwhelmed because he asked, "A lot to take in isn't it?"

"Yeah," I answered with a smile, "it definitely is." I then began to question him a little more about his experiences since then. One of the biggest questions I had related to something he said earlier in the session. He had said that things were going well but still were very hard. From what he told me it sounded like everything was going great. He was learning to deal with his worries and frustration in the moment, and God was beginning to use him to encourage his wife.

"Even though God's word is being spoken into my life," Matt said slowly as he tried to clearly communicate how he felt, "it isn't always easy to believe. I had always thought that once I climbed up the holiness ladder I thought existed, then trusting God would be easier. But it isn't that God wants me to strive harder to do good things and not sin, He wants me to turn to Him. After I trust Him things are good, but it still very hard to trust Him. It goes against all my instincts. I want to do all I can to provide for myself and Michele. I want to have enough money in the bank so I never have to worry. I want to have my house paid off, but God says I am right where He wants me and I have all I need. Therefore I should trust him and relax in the fact that no matter how hard I strive it is still in His hands."

"So God is telling you to relax?" I asked with a smile.

He smiled back and said, "Actually, the word he brought to mind for me was repose. Like I am supposed to get out a lawn chair, get some sun, and spend the day reading his word. As I get to know Him, He will guide me."

"That sounds pretty good," I replied. "We will have to see how it turns out."

Matt headed home after our hour together had come to a close. As he left I realized something about our session that day. Matt didn't seem to come that day for help or encouragement. He didn't really seem to be struggling with an issue that needed help. It was as if he came with the sole purpose of sharing what God had taught him. I was definitely glad he did, yet I was a little awestruck because I had never had a meeting with a client like that before.

Matt left my office that day very encouraged and confident God would provide a job. However, having spent the entire last week job searching definitely waned on his enthusiasm today for going job hunting again. Instead he headed to the grocery store to pick up some food for the week.

While pondering what to buy, he slowly pushed the cart up and down each isle. As he did this, he began thinking about all God had taught him lately. He couldn't remember anytime in his life that he had learned so much about God in such a short time. "God thank you so much for blessing me with the privilege of getting to know you better the last couple weeks. I have enjoyed the time I have got to spend with You while not working. I feel like You have blessed me in a much different way than I would have ever expected. Thank You for the peace You've given me."

After that short prayer, Michele came to his mind. He realized that much of the last couple weeks had been spent worrying about the job situation and working through it himself. He and Michele had talked about it some, but they definitely did not talk about it as much as they probably should have. It suddenly hit him how he had been so concerned with getting through it himself that it had over shadowed him showing love to her.

Turning his cart around, Matt headed back to the produce section. Michele's favorite meal was stir fry, so he decided he would make it for her that evening. He picked out all he needed for the meal and pondered what else he could do for her. "Candles!" He exclaimed out loud. A smile spread across his face as he headed towards the household goods. He even pushed the cart a little faster than 'adults' should and picked his feet up to ride on it. He couldn't remember the last time he had had that feeling of giddy fun.

Michele arrived home for dinner that night to find Matt nicely dressed, her favorite meal on the table, and a couple lit candles on the table. Her head tilted a little to the side and she pulled her hand up to her mouth. A smile then slowly slid across her face as Matt walked toward her. Giving her a kiss, Matt said, "I just wanted to remind you how special you are and that I love you."

Matt and Michele sat around on the couch after dinner that night and talked most of the evening. Matt got a much better understanding of how Michele was processing their situation, and what her biggest stressors were. He was definitely surprised to hear her single biggest worry lately. He had been most worried about money and assumed she would be as well. Although money was on her mind quite often, her biggest concern was that their relationship would begin to suffer as the hardship dragged on. That thought hadn't really occurred to Matt until Michele mentioned it. "Our relationship is way more important to me than our house," she had told him. "I would much rather have to sell the house, live in a trailer, and sell a bunch of stuff than watch our relationship wane and fade away."

That night before they went to bed, Matt and Michele said a long prayer together. They thanked God for how He had provided so far and for promising to continue to provide. They asked for wisdom for the future and that He would continue to draw them closer to Him. As they continued to learn, He definitely did not disappoint them.

Matt's dream that night was different than the rest. In the other dreams he was comfortable with his surroundings. It was as if he knew why he was there or where he was supposed to be walking. Yet this dream brought with it a sense of insecurity. He didn't know why he was there or where he was to be going. For some reason he did not feel like he fit in with all those around him.

Matt found himself in the heart of New York City. He was wandering aimlessly on the sidewalks along with hoards of other people. Cars whizzed past honking at who knows what, and sirens were heard in the distance. The noise of the city filled the air. Around him there was a dull roar of hundreds of people on their cell phones. All of them seemed oblivious to everything going on around them. As Matt watched them all pass by him, he realized that everyone of them seemed the same. They were all on their phones, and all seemed to be in a hurry. Everyone of them talked at such loud volume that it was obvious they weren't concerned with anything but expressing their opinion to the hearer on the receiving side of the call. It was as if they were all in their own personal world.

At one point he stopped walking and just stood in the middle of the sidewalk to see what happened. The steady stream of people seemed to just treat him as a boulder in their path. They would part on his front side then come together again after they passed him.

Very soon, Matt found himself standing at Time Square. Billboards and electronic signs littered the sides of the buildings with ads for cell phones, clothing brands, a record label, a musical, investment companies, beer companies, soft drink companies, and car companies. Matt just stood there for a little while awestruck and overwhelmed by how big everything was as well as how many signs and ads there actually were.

Matt crossed over to what appeared to be an island of buildings between the two streets of cars. Parked up on the curb was a Little Debbie's truck. Matt noticed something was on top of it. He realized it was a couch and someone was sitting up there. He laughed to himself and shook his head thinking it was a little comical. He looked from side to side seeing if anyone else noticed the unusual sight, but none of the others seemed to care if they did notice.

Matt kept his eyes looking up towards the man sitting on top of the truck as Matt walked closer to him. As he drew near, Matt saw that he recognized the man. It was once again Jesus. Jesus was also looking toward him. When they made eye contact Jesus waved him over as if to say, "Come on up!"

Matt walked around to the back of the vehicle. Climbing up onto the bumper, he pulled himself up onto the roof. He then went over and sat on the couch with Jesus. Sitting down on the couch, Matt glanced around. He was now several feet above the crowd and had an even better view of his surroundings. Not only were the sidewalks like constant streams of people, but the roads were like rivers of cars. Except this river appeared mainly yellow because half the cars were cabs.

After sitting there several minutes in silence observing all that was going on, Matt finally began to talk to Jesus. "What are we doing here?" he asked.

"Observing," Jesus said with a smile.

Matt smiled back and said, "Well yeah, but why?"

Jesus' head turned back to facing the street, and he stretched his arm out towards the street with his palm up as if presenting the masses below to Matt. "I wanted you to see this. I wanted you to see what is going on in the world and where you were headed."

Matt looked down at all the people wandering the streets. They did seem oblivious to everything but their own current issues, and they all looked tense and stressed. Other than the people being a little overly self-absorbed, there didn't seem to be any flagrant sinning going on in front of him. No one was getting stabbed, all the people were dressed respectively, no women were too slutty, and even the ads around seemed to be of decent taste.

"Where was I headed?" Matt slowly dragged out of his mouth with a confused look plastered on his face.

Jesus leaned forward and pointed down. "Look at this guy down here." Matt then leaned forward and also looked down at a man leaning against the truck. Jesus continued, "His name is Devon. He has a wife and a one year old at home, and he only makes minimum wage. They live out of the city, but this was the only job he could find. He takes the train an hour into work and an hour home. He also works twelve hours a day. So subtracting out the hours he sleeps a night, he barely sees his wife and son. He is My child, but he rarely talks with Me. He thinks he is too busy."

Jesus then pointed at a blonde woman in dress slacks and a white button down shirt. Normally it would have been impossible to spot exactly who He pointed at in the crowd, but she was currently surrounded by a passing group of men all wearing black suits making her white shirt stand out.

"Her name is Karen," he began again, "She is thirty-four and single. Her parents are believers and have had a relationship with me since she was born. Karen has never really wanted anything to do with Me though. She was always too consumed with the idea of success. She is currently one person below the vice president where she works, but has a minimal life outside of that. Her only free time is filled with yoga or any event where she feels she could increase her business acquaintances."

Jesus then pointed at a cab sitting at the stop light. "That driver is Jamal. He has driven cabs for over thirteen years. He makes enough to live on. He is currently living with his girlfriend. They have lived together for a year now. They fight all the time, but neither wants to leave because they hated living and feeling alone."

Even though the light had turned and the cab had begun to drive away, Jesus looked over at Matt and continued on, "His passenger was a pastor of a mega church from Arizona.

He has written a couple books, and his church continues to grow. He was here in New York City for a conference this week and is now heading home. It has been over two weeks since I have gotten to talk to him." Jesus shook his head with a sad look on his face. "He gets so busy trying to do work for Me that he forgets to be spending time with Me. Yeah he prays here and there, but he doesn't spend the time to listen to what I have to tell him. He even reads in the Word a lot while preparing for sermons or conferences."

"Jesus," Matt interrupted. "I thought that is what You want from us. I thought we are supposed to do those things."

Jesus passionately exclaimed, "You are! I want you to read My word and talk with Me, but it goes deeper than that. It isn't about what you are doing. It is all about the motive."

At this Matt was still a little confused. He understood what Jesus was saying about motive, but the pastor's motives had sounded pretty good. He was trying to lead more people to know Christ. So what could be wrong with that?

After pausing for a moment Jesus looked deep into Matt's eyes and asked, "Why are you here on earth Matt? I mean all of mankind. Why were you created?"

Matt quickly gave the church answer of, "To glorify you Lord."

"True," Jesus said with a smile. "How do you do that though?"

Matt glanced away from Jesus and looked down at the people passing by. "By living in line with what you say and helping others get to know You as well," Matt answered.

Jesus, still looking intently at Matt, repeated Matt's statement but in the form of a question. "By living in line with what I say? What have you been learning the last couple weeks Matt?"

Matt thought back over what God had been teaching him. The first thing that came to mind was all he had learned about being crucified with Christ. He remembered how he had been a slave to sin while in Adam's family, but now he was free from that bondage through his death with Christ. He thought of the life of Christ living inside of him. He began to recall how God desires him to get to know Him first and foremost. Matt recalled times when he would sit down and talk with God, taking the time to listen, and then he would end up having God work through him. Michele, on several occasions, had commented that she could see God working in Matt's life the last couple weeks.

As Matt reminisced over all this, he began to see a reoccurring thought. God's main desire was for him to get to know God. As he did that, he would automatically begin doing the other things like praying and reading the Bible. God didn't want him to just do those things like a checklist for holy living. He wanted Matt to desire and seek to know Him more intently than any other thing.

Matt looked up from his thoughts and saw Jesus smiling at him. "Why are you here on earth Matt?" He asked once again.

"To get to know you," Matt responded.

"That's right." Jesus said. He then looked up towards heaven and said, "This is eternal life, that they may know You, the only true God, and Jesus Christ whom You have sent."[4]

Jesus' eyes slowly returned down from looking up and landed on Matt. "All those people I showed you earlier," gesturing to the crowd, "they are all so busy with what they think is life. They occupy themselves with attaining goods, reputations, respected positions at work, and all sorts of things. Even my children strain themselves over trying to do great things for Me. Could I not command the rocks to cry out and declare My glory? Life is not all this busyness you see around you. It is not growing up, going to college, getting a job, getting married, and having kids. That's not life! Life is getting to know Me! You remember what Adam's punishment was for sinning? Death. He was kicked out of the garden and the human race was separated from My Father. That is why I had to come to die: so that man could once again, through Me, be reconciled and restored to a relationship with My Father and grow in knowledge of Us!"

Matt was now staring intently at Jesus. It had never occurred to him how important the pursuit of knowing God was. After hearing Jesus explain it though, it clearly made sense. Everything Matt experienced throughout his years on earth he now understood was the way God taught him things. He thought back on years of struggling off and on with depression. 'I was created to continually seek to know God more. When I would get so weighed down with worries and demeaning thoughts, I wouldn't seek to know God at all. Actually, I couldn't because I never allowed myself to see past myself and my hurts,' Matt thought to himself.

As he thought about that, he understood his depression a little more. 'It was a side effect of the bigger issue. Deep down I knew I was missing out on something because life just seemed so pointless. I was missing out on the pursuit of knowing God and the joy God promises will come from Him.'

Matt's thoughts then went to his recent hardships with losing his job. 'God brought this hardship into my life to show me what life truly is. If I hadn't lost my job then I would have continued living the same way I had for years. By losing my job, I turned to God because I was finally at the end of myself and my ideas.'

As all these thoughts raced through Matt's brain, he suddenly looked up at Jesus and asked, "I lost my job so that I would learn all of this didn't I?" Jesus just nodded his head agreeing. Matt then looked out on the sea of people and continued, "I would have just floated through life like the rest of these people knowing I was hurting but unaware of what I was missing." With that he looked back over at Jesus and said, "Thank you Lord."

VERSE REFRENCES

1) **Philippians 1:21**
2) **Matthew 11:28-29**
3) **Matthew 6:25-34**
4) **John 17:3**

CHAPTER EIGHT

Over the next few weeks, a lot of things took place in Matt and Michele's lives. Michele graduated with her degree in social work, but she decided to stay at her job until Matt secured full-time work. Matt started mowing their church's huge yard for $75 a week, and their neighbor Harold started paying Matt $25 a week to mow his yard. Matt even got hired by someone from his small group to set up a small computer network at his business. Even though it only took two days to do, Matt still got paid well for it.

Although Matt had some part time work with mowing and other odd jobs, he still kept praying and searching for full-time work. Finally, now a month and a half after losing his job, Matt had his first job interview. Michele and he were both super excited. Maybe God was going to provide a full-time job! The day before and the day of the interview Matt was elated. He was a little nervous knowing that it was in a field he had never worked before, but he was confident that God provides.

The interview, Matt thought, went really well. He had been poised, confident, and, due to preparation, had been able to answer questions related to the new job field formally unknown to him. A couple days went by without hearing from them. Matt called to check up on the status. The company informed him that they were still considering all the applicants.

Matt's confidence had begun to diminish after a whole week had passed. His prayers began to get a little shorter and his anxiety began to grow. Finally, he heard their answer. They had chosen someone else.

Matt sat on the couch dumbfounded at the news he had just received. God promised to provide for him and Michele. He was approaching two months without a job. God can do anything. Why wouldn't He just give him a job? "Yeah, I have learned a ton," Matt began to say to himself, "but why do I have to continue on in this hardship? I am sick of all this!"

Matt felt the Holy Spirit tug on his heart saying, "Trust me. I will provide. Look to Me because I want to teach you more through this. Open my word, and you will find your peace once again." "No," Matt said out loud, "I don't feel like it. I am frustrated and feel like you let me down today God."

With that he headed to his now finished patio with a glass of lemonade and a book to read. He was determined not to think about all that happened. Where he sat was shaded by a large tree, but it was still very hot outside. He sat out there about an hour reading in the book. Many pages he would have to read several times, because while he read he constantly knew the Holy Spirit was trying to talk to him. He would just force himself to concentrate on the book more and reread what he had just read purposely ignoring the Holy Spirit's voice.

The day dragged on and Matt's stress grew. When Michele arrived home that evening, she asked him if he had heard from the job that day. He told her about not getting the job. Shaking his head he began to rant out his frustrations. "I don't understand why God didn't give me this job. He promises to provide, and we have been patiently waiting! Why doesn't He just provide already?

Why do we have to wait so long to see what He is going to do? God causes all things to work together for good for those who love Him, so why isn't He allowing this good into our life?" Michele shrugged and answered that she didn't know.

Their evening was far from enjoyable. Michele knew Matt was hurting and disappointed, and Matt felt like God had failed him. After a night of TV, they both headed to bed.

Matt now stood on the edge of a stream. The stream had a little gleam as it reflected the small bit of sun not hid by clouds. All around Matt were tons of little flat stones perfect for skipping. So he decided to pick a few up and give it a try. After skipping the forth or fifth stone, he noticed the stream was beginning to shine much more. Looking up he saw the sky opening up as the clouds spread. It got so bright that he could no longer look up. He could not even look at the water any longer. He just sat down on a big stone and stared at the ground squinting.

"Matt," he heard from the sky, "why are you so frustrated with Me?"

Knowing it was God talking to him, he began to answer, "You promised to provide for me, but no matter how long I have waited I still haven't gotten a job."

"Have I not provided for you?" God asked.

At this Matt bit his teeth together still being frustrated and replied, "Well yeah, you have given us enough to live on."

After a short pause, God asked, "So what's the problem then?"

Matt's talking then went from a frustrated rant to more of a self pitying monolog. "I just want a job. I am tired of constantly not knowing where money is going to come from each month. In Romans, you promise to work all things for good to those who love You. How is it good that I don't have a job when so many other people who never even think about you have great jobs?"

God asked Matt if he knew what followed that verse. Matt thought about it for a second and had to admit he didn't know. God then began to quote the passage, "And we know that God causes all things to work together for good to those who love God, to those who are called according to His purpose. For those whom He foreknew, He also predestined to become conformed to the image of His Son, so that He would be the firstborn among the brethren."[1]

God paused for a second before He began explaining the passage. "I work all things for good to those who love Me. Those who love Me believe I know what is best and that I will work My purpose through them. My purpose is to conform you to the image of My son, Jesus. You remember how you have the life of Christ living inside of you? You remember how you learned that these hardships have taught you to know Me more? And last of all, do you remember how, when you got to know Me more, more of Jesus' life was revealed in you? That is why you have gone through so many hardships lately. I want good for you, but it isn't the good you have always thought. The best thing possible for you is that you would be conformed, or changed, to the image of Jesus. Hardships allow you to trust Me, learn about Me, and therefore grow in knowledge of Me. Knowing more about your God allows you to better reflect Him to the world. The more you reflect Christ's life residing inside of you, the more you will reveal Him to the world. The more you reveal Him to the world then the more you glorify Me. The more you glorify me, the more you are doing what you were created for. What could be better for you then doing what you were created for?

"I know hardships are not fun, but sometimes they truly are what's best for you. You will have a job when it is in your best interest to have a job."

All this seemed like a ton for Matt to take in. Yet at the same time all that God had said did make sense to him. Inside of him still arose a desire to fight a little against God's explanation. What he was going through was so hard, and Matt was beginning to feel God had overstepped His promise of not to bring more hardships into a believer's life than he could bear. "You promised you wouldn't give me more than I can bear," Matt began, "and I already got to that point today. I am beyond frustrated and I do not have the patience to wait any longer for a job."

"You not knowing all I have done for you does not equal Me breaking a promise," God replied.

Matt, forgetting how bright the sky was, began to look up questioningly. His eyes began to sting instantly, and he whipped his head back down to the ground and said, "What do you mean?"

At that question God began to quote the passage, "Grace and peace be multiplied to you in the knowledge of God and of Jesus our Lord; seeing that His divine power has granted to us everything pertaining to life and godliness, through the knowledge of Him who called us by His own glory and excellence."[2] Continuing on God said, "I have given you everything you need for life and godliness. That includes patience and endurance. Therefore you have the patience to get through this hardship. The truth is, you just don't want to be patient anymore because it is getting hard. Don't you remember what My word says about hardships? Exult in your tribulations, knowing that tribulation brings about perseverance; and perseverance, proven character; and proven character, hope, and hope does not disappoint, because My love has been poured out in your heart through the Holy Spirit.[3]

"I want you to learn to put all of your hope in Me. I don't enjoy seeing you go through this hard time, but the finished project of you being conformed to Jesus' image will be well worth it. Consider the peace, joy, and comfort you have found in Me as you went through these hardships. Did you ever have that before even when you had a full-time job?"

Matt knew he hadn't. There was an aspect of the peace and comfort that he had felt lately that only came from putting his trust in God. No amount of money could replace knowing that God will provide for all his needs. As Matt began to recall the last month or so, he realized how much his mood had changed and the joy he had. He couldn't recall a time in years past that he had truly been joyful. He had been happy of course, but each time that had been based on circumstances. He had never before found joy even while going through hard circumstances. As Matt recollected all of this, he knew it was all because of his growing relationship with God. There was no other explanation possible.

Despite knowing this, something inside of Matt's heart still desired to harden his heart against God. Matt still longed for a job and for financial security. 'I just want to allow myself to vent for a while. Then I will turn back to God,' Matt thought to himself.

God knew all of the thoughts circling through Matt's brain and so he said, "Matt, sin is crouching at your door step. If you do not master it, then it will master you. You know that the self pity, frustration, and anger that you are considering to allowing your heart, even if you say it is only temporary, will effect your relationship with Me. Jesus' death and resurrection freed you from the power of sin in your life so you could walk in newness of life and walk with Me continually. If you chose to willfully walk into what you know I command you not to do then it will break our fellowship."

At this Matt was a little confused. He thought God viewed Christ's righteousness instead of his sin now. Therefore, how could Matt's sin effect his relationship with God the Father?

God answered his thoughts saying, "I chose before the foundation of the world that I would view you in Christ and on account of His righteousness so that you could have unbroken fellowship and an ongoing relationship with Me. I knew that you would still give in to your sinful flesh from Adam at times and that would break our fellowship. But now, whenever you unknowingly sin, it will not break our fellowship. As you walk with Me and get to know Me, I will use the Holy Spirit to convict you of the sin you committed. When you admit your sin, change your actions, and possibly apologize to someone if I ask you to, then you can continue to walk in unbroken fellowship with Me. But when you are convicted by the Holy Spirit to change your actions or thoughts, like you are convicted now, and if you do not repent and change your actions then that fellowship will be broken."

This explanation sounded pretty serious to Matt. He didn't fully grasp exactly what it meant, but God continued on with His explanation a little further. "You are my child now and will be for all eternity because your salvation is based on the blood of Jesus and not on your ability to live in line with what I say. However, your relationship here on earth with Me is based on your obedience to Me and your listening to the Spirit's voice in your life. If you chose not to listen, then you will wander into darkness and death. Eternal life is knowing Me. If you do not seek Me constantly, then you won't be living. You will be willfully walking back to the heartache and pain you used to experience daily."

Matt was beginning to feel torn. He knew the absolute truth of what God spoke. He could feel the Holy Spirit convicting him and telling him to turn his heart back to submission to God. He knew trusting God and giving up his fears and worries was what God commanded of him right now, but he didn't want to say, 'I trust you and understand this hardship will be for my good.' Matt was tired of being unsure where his finances would come from every month. He wished so badly that God would just give him a job; then Matt thought it would be so much easier to turn back and trust God again.

God left Matt on the rocky banks of the stream with one last thought, "Matt, walking with me is not always easy, but I have promised to give you everything you need to do it. I chose to have you crucified with Christ so that you would pass from death to life. You passed from Adam to Christ. You have eternal life now, yet it is your choice whether you will get to know Me in this life and experience that eternal life here on earth. Jesus told the world that He came that you all may have life and have it abundantly.[4] If eternal life was just life that lasted forever, then how could you have more of it? How could you have an abundant amount of something that by definition lasts forever? It is because eternal life is so much more than living forever. I don't like the illustration that so many people use when trying to explain eternal life. In front of a big group of people, they will point to the two sides of the room and say, 'the wall on the left side of the room is the beginning of creation and the wall on the other side of the room is eternity.' Then, holding up a needle they say, 'your life is represented by the tip of this needle. That is how small your life is in view of eternity.' The illustration is true, but it leaves out so much more! Eternal life is not only quantitative; it is equally qualitative! Imagine a never ending line at your feet that goes on forever. That is how long eternal life will last. Now image a never ending line that goes straight up. That is how much you can enjoy eternal life. The more you get to know Me then the more you will enjoy life.

"Matt, I promise you joy and peace. It is your choice whether you will experience it. You are about to have your last influential dream Matt. You now know why you are on earth and how to walk with Me. You no longer need Me to speak to you in dreams. I have given you my Word in the Bible, and My Spirit resides inside of you to convict and teach you my ways. What is required by you now is that you walk daily by faith believing what I say is true."

With that the voice subsided. Once again the brightness around Matt began to grow. It got so bright that he could no longer keep his eyes open even staring down at the rocks. He squeezed his eyes closed as tight as possible yet the light still seemed to burn. All of sudden he realized that a breeze could now be felt pushing against his face and hair. The light then began to fade, and Matt squinted his eyes less and less. Finally, he was able to open them again, but he was no longer on the bank of a stream.

VERSE REFRENCES

1) **Romans 8:28-29**
2) **II Peter 1:2-3**
3) **Romans 5:3-5**
4) **John 10:10**

CHAPTER NINE

Matt was now at the helm of an old wooden ship. The ship appeared to be straight out of an old sailing movie. It had massive sails thrusting the boat forward and a numerous amount of crew members attending to various tasks. The ships captain stood beside him wearing what appeared to be an admiral's cap.

Matt scanned the magnificent views of the ocean surrounding him on every side. As far as he could see, there was nothing but crystal clear water surrounding the ship for miles. A cloudless blue sky stretched across the atmosphere above, and an unusually bright sun beat its rays down onto the water. The whole scene seemed almost to be too picturesque and serene. There were even a couple dolphins following alongside the starboard side of the ship.

Matt began to stroll along the deck of the ship admiring the hard work of the sailors. They all seemed to be doing their daily tasks without a complaint. One was mending fishing nets while another folded up a net that had already been sown. Several men were on their hands and knees scrubbing the deck in an attempt to clean it. Overhead there was a man who appeared to be tightening the sails, and another man was far above in a basket looking through a telescope for what lay ahead.

After taking a long stroll around the ship, Matt headed back to where the captain was standing. "Where we headed?" asked Matt.

The captain looked over at Matt with a surprised look and asked, "What do you mean?"

Matt was a little confused by the captain's reply and further elaborated his question. "I mean where is this ship going? Where is our destination?"

The captain once again glanced at Matt with a puzzled look. "We are at our destination," the captain slowly replied still peering at Matt as if he was clueless.

Matt contorted his face for a second showing that he was still very much confused by the statement. His mind attempted to come up with thoughts of what the captain could have meant. 'Maybe he meant that we are on course to where we are going, and thus we are where we want to be,' Matt thought to himself. Unable to decide what the captain had meant Matt just blurted out, "I'm sorry, but I do not understand what you mean. We are on a ship in the middle of the ocean. We are surrounded by water. We have to have some destination that we are headed to!"

The captain glanced at Matt a second and looked up to the sky. Looking back at Matt he made eye contact and pointed to the sun.

"We... are going to the sun?" Matt asked in a cynical tone.

The captain shook his head back and forth and said, "No, we are in the light!" As a smile slid across his face, he continued, "Look around you. There isn't a cloud in the sky, the water is crystal clear, and the sun is shinning bright. Where we are right now is exactly where we want to be!"

Matt was a little caught off guard by the captain's response. In his mind there must always be a destination because the ships crew couldn't survive indefinitely out on open water. The captain noticed that Matt was in deep thought and decided to elaborate his earlier answer a little more in depth. "It's not like we are going to stay in this one spot forever. We just docked on an island three days ago and have enough food to survive us till the next time we dock. Our only task is to stay in the light and follow it where it leads us."

'That is a little unusual,' Matt thought to himself. He began to smile as he asked the captain, "So is this like a vacation cruise for you guys?"

"Vacation?" the captain repeated. "No, this is definitely not a vacation. It's just the way life is. Who wouldn't want to be constantly in the sun instead of trudging through storms or bad weather?"

"True," Matt responded as he began to think about all the hardships he had encountered in his life recently. They felt as if they were little personal storms for him to go through.

"So how do you manage to stay in the sun all the time?" Matt asked.

"Well," the captain replied, "It is impossible to avoid the storms. They just blow up out of nowhere sometimes. But the haze on the other hand, that is a choice."

Matt looked puzzlingly at the captain and repeated, "The haze?"

The captain continued on, "Yeah. You know, well, have you heard of the sirens?"

"The singing mermaids?" Matt asked.

"Yes, the singing mermaids. When we hear their songs they tug at our desires to steer the ship towards them. They sing songs telling us how wonderful we are and how much we deserve. Every time we hear them, their flattery and promises sound so good and so true. They make us feel that they will fulfill all of our deepest desires. However, when we seek after them we leave our path laid out by the sun. By choosing to follow their voices, our boat gets submerged into a foggy haze. Their voices take control of our thoughts and moods, and it is a struggle to come back to the sun. Their words consume our thoughts, and we reside in the haze for days."

Shaking his head as a serious look came across his face, the captain continued, "A lot of ships have been shipwrecked because of the haze. Many captains are still aimlessly guiding their ships in the haze meditating on the words of the sirens.

"Storms, on the other hand, are unavoidable. They come out of nowhere, and the captain has no choice but to go through them."

Thinking about what the captain had said, Matt asked, "So how do you get out of them?"

"Well," the captain replied, "Before we get thrust into a storm we are headed in the right direction. We know where the sun is, and since we are already heading toward it, we just continue on track. The sun doesn't go anywhere when the storms arise. We just can not see it behind the clouds. We have never been let down by seeking the sun during a storm. It has always brought us through."

Matt thought about all the captain had said. It made a lot of sense to him. Thanking the captain for the explanations, he began to take a walk around the ship as thoughts of light and darkness floated around in his mind. When he had gotten to the front side of the ship, he saw a man lying on a lounge chair who appeared to be sun tanning. "What are you up to?" Matt asked.

The man looked up at him with a smile and said, "Reposing."

"Relaxing hmm? Good day for that," Matt said back to the man. As he replied he began to observe the man more closely. He had dark hair, tan skin, and had a huge bushy beard at least five inches long. It was so bushy that the man's face was mostly hidden, but Matt could still see a smile beaming through the rough growth of facial hair.

"John," the man said introducing himself and sticking his hand out to shake Matt's.

"I'm Matt," Matt replied to him.

"Nice to meet you Matt," John said back. "Please take a seat next to me and join in." This seemed like a pretty enjoyable idea to Matt so he took a seat in the lounger next to him.

Once he had taken a seat, John began talking again. "So," pausing a second, "God told me that this was going to be your last dream through which he speaks to you."

"He told you that?" Matt asked surprised.

"Yeah," John continued, "He sent me to explain a couple more things to you. I am the same John who was Jesus' disciple. You know the one who wrote the books in the Bible: the gospel of John, first, second and third John, and Revelation."

'Whoa,' Matt thought. 'I wonder if he will tell me a bunch of stories about being around Jesus.' Matt just sat there and stared at John.

John smiled and said, "You must be used to talking to Jesus in your dreams. He usually hears your thoughts and answers you. I, on the other hand, cannot do that. So you have to actually ask me things."

Matt laughed a little and then asked, "So why did God send you?"

"I came to help explain in a little more detail some of the things God told you. Mainly, I was sent to talk about what God taught me and what I wrote in the book of I John. Ever read it?"

"Yup," Matt replied.

"Good," John said, "Then you have a groundwork for what I am about to tell you. You see, the purpose of the book was to help other believers better understand fellowship."

"Fellowship?" Matt asked.

"Yeah, think of it as an unbroken, ongoing, constant relationship. When I wrote the book, the believers looked up to us apostles because of our relationship with God and our knowledge of Him. They desired to be in fellowship with us, because they knew we were in fellowship with God. That's why I said, 'What we have seen and heard we proclaim to you also, so you too may have fellowship with us; and indeed our fellowship is with the Father, and with His Son Jesus Christ. These things we write, so that our joy may be made complete.'[1] I wrote to tell the believers all that God had taught me about fellowship with Him and of the joy that it brings.

"All right, that makes sense. So what do I need to know?" Matt asked.

"You know when you are tempted to do something that God commands you not to do? That is when you are presented with the choice of staying in fellowship with God or not. You see, 'God is light, and in Him there is no darkness at all.'[2] So just like the captain of this ship is constantly seeking to stay in the light, you too are to constantly stay in the light."

Matt confusingly looked at John and asked him to elaborate. "Sin is darkness Matt. God is completely light and cannot be in the presence of sin. Therefore when you are convicted by the Holy Spirit that something is sin and then you chose to do it anyways, you are no longer walking in the light. You are no longer in fellowship with God."

"Wait a minute," Matt said. His facial expression clearly showed that he was deep in thought. He asked, "You are saying my sin breaks my relationship with God? I thought Jesus blood paid for my sin and made it possible for me to have a relationship."

"That is completely true, Matt," John replied. "But I am not talking about being saved from the punishment of sin which you know as hell. I am talking about being saved from the power of sin in your life. You know that you used to be a slave to sin and through being baptized into Christ's death you were freed from that slavery. You no longer have to sin and you can constantly have a continual ongoing relationship with God. When you choose to do something that you know is sin, then that constant relationship is broken. It doesn't change the fact that you are still God's child and will spend eternity with Him, but your relationship here on earth is put on stand still while you willfully sin, because when you are in the darkness you cannot be in the light."

Matt's mind began to take in all that John had just told him. He began to filter it through what the captain had told him. "So this darkness, it is just like the haze the captain told me about isn't it? It is a choice to go into the haze, and the captain has to change course from following the light to go into it."

John shook his head in agreement. "All that the sirens promise are things of the world: happiness, success, and all the possessions you could ever imagine. Man desires to get all he wants, which is the lust of the flesh. Man desires all he sees, which is the lust of the eyes. Also, man desires success, power, and popularity, which are the boastful pride of life. Seeking these things draws man away from God. That is why I wrote, 'Do not love the world or the things in the world. If anyone loves the world, the love of the Father is not in him. For all that is in the world, the lust of the flesh and the lust of the eyes and the boastful pride of life, is not of the Father, but is from the world. The world is passing away, and also its lusts; but the one who does the will of God lives forever.'"[3]

Matt considered all John had just said. 'Sinning breaks fellowship,' he thought to himself. Thinking about it, he realized there were times he would sin without realizing at the time that it was sin. One instance he thought of was an incident that happened at a small group one evening. The discussion got a little heated, and Matt got rather upset at his friend's opinion. Being caught up in the moment Matt had heatedly explained why his friend was wrong. The next day he felt the Holy Spirit convict him that he had not acted in love. "You might have been right about the doctrinal issue, but your anger caused you to act unloving. Also, the argument was more about saving your pride than about accurately explaining My word," the Holy Spirit had put into his mind. He apologized to God for his pride and was also led by the Holy Spirit to apologize to his friend.

Matt asked John about the situation. "So I understand willfully going against what God says breaks fellowship, but what about when you do it not even realizing it is sin at the time?"

John began his answer by quoting the verse, "Beloved, if our heart does not condemn us, we have confidence before God."[4] Continuing on he began to explain it, "God gives us His word in the Bible so we would know what He commands. He also gives us the Holy Spirit to reside inside of us and remind us of His truth and to convict us of our sin. A believer's conscience is the Holy Spirit's voice into his life. It is not the sin that breaks fellowship with God. It is the willful choice to ignore the Holy Spirit's voice that breaks fellowship. If you choose to willfully sin when you know it is wrong that breaks fellowship with God, but if you are convicted of a sin you have already committed then you are presented with a similar choice. You can either repent of the thing you now know is sin, or you can refuse to listen to the Holy Spirit and choose to walk in the darkness that is sin."

Matt felt like he was beginning to understand what was said, but just in case, he thought he should clarify it with John. "God told me earlier to be careful because sin was crouching at my door. What He was saying was in that moment my flesh wanted to do something that I knew God commanded I shouldn't. If I would have sinned knowing it was sin then I would have broken fellowship. I would have chosen to indulge in what my flesh wanted and thus shown that I love the world more than God. Is that correct?"

John nodded and made a final point, "Choosing to walk in fellowship with God is a daily choice. You choose daily if you will do what He commands, yet if you are not constantly reading His word then how will you know if your life lines up with what He commands? As you get to know Him and seek Him, then and only then, will your joy and peace grow as you experience fellowship with Him."

Matt, up to this point, was leaning forward in his seat intently listening to John. He now slid back in his chair and sighed. It was amazing all God had done for him. By God's grace he was saved from the penalty of sin, hell, and through being baptized by the Spirit into Christ's death he was also saved from the power of sin in his life. God had taught him how to constantly walk with Him while Matt was still on earth and still going to sin. God had even ordained that truly unknown sin in a believer's life would not break fellowship with God, but of course ignored sin is not the same as unknown sin.

"I think I finally understand what Romans 1:16-17 means," Matt began to say to John. "'For I am not ashamed of the gospel, for it is the power of God for salvation to everyone who believes, to the Jew first and also to the Greek. For in it the righteousness of God is revealed from faith to faith; as it is written, but the righteous man shall live by faith.'[5] I was saved from hell by faith in Jesus Christ. In the same way as I daily walk by faith, God now saves me from the power that sin used to have over me. I have to constantly believe that sin has no power over me, and that the Holy Spirit will reveal any sin in my life. Doing these things allows me to have an unbroken relationship with God while I am still on earth!"

John just smiled at Matt and leaned back in his chair. "Looks like my time with you is up," he said, "It was nice to meet you."

As he said that, Matt looked up and realized they were about to go under a huge bridge. Matt had been so engulfed in the conversation that he had not even noticed they were headed towards one. As the boat drifted under the bridge, Matt saw a rope ladder hanging from it.

"That is your way up," John said with a smile.

"Thanks," Matt said pausing for a second, "God definitely used you to help me understand His word much more thoroughly." Matt then grabbed the rope ladder and began to climb up it.

The bridge was rather tall, and at times Matt was pretty scared at the height he was climbing. After several minutes of climbing he finally reached the top and pulled himself over the railing. After climbing over the railing, he saw a man waiting for him.

VERSE REFRENCES

1) **I John 1:3-4**
2) **I John 1:5**
3) **I John 2:15-17**
4) **I John 3:19**
5) **Romans 1:16-17**

CHAPTER TEN

"I'm Paul," the man said sticking out his hand to shake Matt's.

"Let me guess," Matt said with a smile, "The Paul who used to be Saul and wrote a lot of the New Testament."

"That would be me!" Paul replied and smiled back.

"God sent you to talk to me about something didn't he?"

"He sure did." Guiding Matt with his hand he implied which direction to walk. They headed towards an island which was probably about a mile away. Once they began walking, Paul continued talking. "I am here to talk about the frustration you had when you got frustrated and mad at God. You remember what it was?" Paul asked.

"Oh course," Matt sheepishly replied, "Not having a job."

"Why where you so frustrated?"

"Well," Matt answered, "Because I know God promises to provide, and I felt like he wasn't. I lost my job a while ago and still haven't found another one."

"God has provided for all your needs though, correct?" Paul asked.

"Yeah," Matt slowly replied while his head slowly dropped to look at his feet.

"Matt, God promises to provide for your needs and to do what is best for you; He doesn't promise you a full time job," Paul said. "If you want to know what else he promises just take a look at the scriptures, 'All who desire to live godly in Christ Jesus will be persecuted.'[1] God doesn't promise health and wellness. Instead He promises hardship will come to those who follow Him.

Matt glanced over at Paul with a perturbed look. "That doesn't sound right. God promises rest for our soul, joy, peace, and," pausing for few seconds while he thought, "other stuff like that."

"Do any of those things require you to be healthy or well off financially?" Paul asked.

Matt thought about it for a minute. Joy and peace he had actually only experienced in the time since he lost his job. The same was true of rest. Rest isn't found from having a job and financial security; it only comes from knowing God is in complete control. "No, I guess I just thought those verses implied God would keep me healthy and financially provided for."

"God will definitely keep you provided for in every way you need, but His definition of what we need is very different than ours."

"How does God decipher if we need something?" Matt asked. "Also, I have always thought the rest He promises would be relaxing, like I wouldn't have to worry. I kind of thought walking with God would take away hardships and make life easier."

At that Paul chuckled a little. "Easier? No. Better? Absolutely yes. Take a look at Moses for an example. 'By faith Moses, when he had grown up, refused to be called the son of Pharaoh's daughter, choosing rather to endure ill-treatment with the people of God than to enjoy the passing pleasures of sin.'[2] By desiring to walk with God, Moses had to give up the easy life of living in Pharaoh's palace. He knew that the future treasures of God would be much more fulfilling than a comfortable sin filled life. By faith Moses considered the reproach of Christ to be of far greater value than the treasures of Egypt.[3] He set his eyes on the future joy to come and not on the hardships he encountered at that time.

"You see Matt, God does everything for our good. Our true good, which a lot of times does not seem to be what we think is good for us. What is truly good for us is everything that will conform us to the image of His Son. The closer we grow to Him, the more of Christ's life will be revealed in us. Many times hardships are necessary to help us see past this world and to put our hope and trust in Him. Some have been tortured, 'not accepting their release, so that they might obtain a better resurrection; and others experienced mockings and scourgings, yes, also chains and imprisonment. They were stoned, they were sawn in two, they were tempted, they were put to death with the sword; they went about in sheepskins, in goatskins, being destitute, afflicted, ill-treated (men of whom the world was not worthy), wandering in deserts and mountains and caves and holes in the ground.'[4] They were willing to go through all these things because they knew that they were just strangers and exiles on this earth. They lived their lives in light of their heavenly home to come. 'Therefore God is not ashamed to be called their God; for He has prepared a city for them.'[5]

"Also, take a look at my life! I have been imprisoned, 'beaten times without number, often in danger of death. Five times I received the Jews thirty-nine lashes. Three times I was beaten by rods, once I was stoned, three times I was shipwrecked, a night and a day I have spent in the deep. I have been on frequent journeys, in danger of rivers, danger from robbers, danger from my countrymen, dangers from the Gentiles, dangers in the city, dangers in the wilderness, dangers in the sea, dangers among false brethren; I have been in labor and hardship, through many sleepless nights, in hunger and thirst, often without food, in cold and exposure.'[6] All of that I received for walking with God. My life would have been WAY easier if I hadn't walked with

God and sought to serve Him, but," he paused as a huge smile slid across his face, "I would have missed out on so much more than I could have ever imagined."

"Like what?" Matt asked.

"When you experience the joy of knowing God nothing can compare. No matter how terrible the circumstances, nothing can take away the peace and joy that comes from God. Nothing on this earth can compare to what we get from Him. Things of this world just detract from our desire to know Christ. 'I count all things to be loss in view of the surpassing value of knowing Christ Jesus my Lord, for whom I have suffered the loss of all things, and count them but rubbish so that I may gain Christ.'[7] I devoted my life to get to know Christ more and to help others know Him more as well. I suffered hardship after hardship for it, but I got to know our God in a way that would have been impossible if I hadn't gone through all of that. I would do it all over a million times if given the chance."

Matt looked at Paul with admiration. How could someone go through so much and be positive about all of the hardships he encountered. "What kept you going during the hard times?" Matt asked.

"The desire 'that I may know Him, and the power of His resurrection and fellowship of His sufferings, being conformed to His death; in order that I may attain to the resurrection from the dead.'"[8]

Matt looked at Paul with a confused look as if to say, "All that went over my head."

Paul then explained all he had said, "My desire was that I may know Him and see his power working through me. I desired this so intently that my desire was summed up as an attempt to attain the resurrection from the dead. In that, I mean I wanted to walk so closely with God here on earth that it would parallel what my relationship with Him will be after my body is resurrected from the dead and I spend eternity with Him. I wanted to be in perfect fellowship with Him untainted by sin.

"I never obtained it or became perfect on your side of eternity, but I pressed on.[9] Matt, use my life as an example for how to live. Many people may profess to love Christ and follow Him, but truth be told their god is their appetite, their glory is in their shame, and they set their minds on earthly things, and their end will be destruction.[10] Do not live like them. 'For our citizenship is in heaven, from which also we eagerly wait for a Savior, the Lord Jesus Christ; who will transform the body of our humble state into conformity with the body of His glory.'[11] Matt, you as a believer have much more to look forward to than a comfortable life here on earth. When Christ returns for his church, they will be transformed into complete conformity with His body. Your life here on earth should be dedicated to getting to know God and through that being conformed to the image of His Son. Look forward to the fact that when Christ returns, your body will be completely conformed and changed to be like Christ's resurrected body. You will be forever saved from the presence of sin. It will no longer taint our relationship with our God in anyway. In the same way that faith saved you from the punishment of sin, and faith saved you from the power of sin in your life now, you can have faith that God will save you from the presence of sin forever. The joy and peace you experience here on earth is a fraction of what you will experience in your relationship with God once sin is forever abolished.

This was quite a lot for Matt to take in. Paul's main desire in life was to get to know Christ and to see Him work through him. He thought of everything in this life as useless compared to the value of getting to know God. Paul knew he would encounter hardship after hardship, but he also knew that he wasn't living for glory in this life. Matt thought about the passage Paul wrote in I Corinthians. "Momentary, light affliction is producing for us an eternal weight of glory far beyond all comparison, while we look not at the things which are seen; for the things which are seen are temporal, but the things which are not seen are eternal."[12] Paul even later compared his earthly body to a temporary dwelling like a tent. He truly did live his life through faith based on what was to come after his death. Paul said in the next chapter in Corinthians, "We have as our ambition," whether on earth or in heaven, "to be pleasing to Him. For we must all appear before the judgment seat of Christ, so that each one may be recompensed for his deeds in the body, according to what he has done, whether good or bad."[13] Paul knew that his whole eternity after death would be spent glorifying God, and Paul lived his life doing that on earth as well. Paul knew we would be held accountable for how we lived. Although believers do not have to fear the great white throne of judgment that nonbelievers will stand before, believers will face the judgment seat of Christ. God's grace was poured out through Christ so that we could walk with Him here on earth and spend eternity with Him. Matt was beginning to realize that to not walk with Christ here on earth would be such a waste of the life that God had given him.

"So life isn't going to be easy, but it will be well worth it." Matt stated.

"That's right," Paul agreed. "Once someone experiences the joy of getting to know Christ intimately then they will understand how nothing on this earth can compare. They will also begin to understand the unfathomable experience of knowing God in perfect harmony that awaits us after this world is gone. So many people profess to believe in Christ's finished work on the cross just because they fear the wrath of God and don't want to go to hell. But if someone truly believes that Christ can save them from eternity in hell, why wouldn't he believe that Jesus will fulfill His promise that any life lived for His glory will bring abundant joy? In the pursuit of God there is no excuse for laziness, apathy, or indifference. If someone actually believes God is worth living for then their life will show it."

Looking straight into Matt's eyes, Paul said, "We are 'born again to a living hope through the resurrection of Jesus Christ from the dead.'[14] In the same way He was resurrected from the dead, God will resurrect our bodies as well. 'We know that when he appears, we will be like Him.'[15] Therefore because of what we have to look forward to, 'set your mind on things above, not on things that are on the earth.'[16] You are to live to obtain an inheritance which is imperishable and undefiled and will not fade away, reserved in heaven for you, who are protected by the power of God through faith. In this you should greatly rejoice, though now for a little while, if necessary, you have been distressed by various trials, so that the proof of your faith, which is more precious than gold, even though tested by fire, may be found to result in praise and glory and honor at the revelation of Jesus Christ.[17] Matt, fix your eyes on Jesus and pursue getting to know Him over everything else. Remember that this world and all that is in it will pass away. So living to obtain anything of this world is futile. Constantly listen to the Spirit and learn to grow in grace."

"Grow in grace?" Matt interrupted.

"Yeah, 'we are God's workmanship, created in Christ Jesus for good works, which God prepared beforehand that we would walk in them.'[18] Christ's life now lives in us, and as we get to know Him, He will live His live through us producing good works. God's grace to us in this instance is that it is not us doing the good works; He is doing good works through us. When you walk in the Spirit, it is no longer you living, but Him living through you. For you have been crucified with Christ; and it is no longer you who live, but Christ lives in you; and the life which you now live in the flesh you should live by faith in the Son of God, who loved you and gave Himself up for you."[19]

At that they both stopped. They had reached the shore and there was now a large gate in front of them. "I am going to have to leave you here Matt. Bodies don't reside where I am going, only our spirits. I won't get my resurrected body till you do. But none the less, this is goodbye for now." The gate opened slowly and Paul walked in. As the door slid shut, Matt heard him yell out from the other side, "Nothing can compare to a life devoted to knowing Christ, set your hope on all He has promised you! Live by faith!"

Well, this is the end of Matt's story for now. It has been a couple months since his last dream, but that doesn't seem to bother him at all. When I asked him about it he said, "God speaks to me through His word and the Holy Spirit. I don't need Him to speak to me in dreams." Matt still does not have a full-time job, but he does have more joy and peace about his current situation than I thought was possible. God has continued to be faithful providing finances by odd jobs for him.

What amazes me most about Matt is how his love for God has grown during this prolonged time of hardship. Watching Matt grow closer to God, even though his circumstances are what they are, has been convicting to me. I realized that for years I have prayed for safety, health, and financial security. My whole life I have wanted a comfortable life more than I have wanted to get to know God. God used Matt's depression to teach him that there is no joy and no peace to be found in this world apart from God. God also used Matt losing his job to teach him that the only secure thing in the universe is God Himself.

My prayer is that Matt's story will impact you in the same way it impacted me. My goal in life up to this point was definitely not to pursue a more intimate and unbroken relationship with Christ. However, seeing Matt's transformation has shown me the impact that it can have. In the last month Matt has had more peace of mind about finances than me, and he doesn't even have a job! I am starting to see that God allows hardships in our lives to draw us closer to Him. All He is doing is allowing our false security in the things of this world to be broken. Though it is hard when it happens, we then see that God alone is the rock which we can turn to. I can now clearly see the truth in the verse, 'But the righteous man shall live by faith,'[20] because living by faith is how the world sees us put our trust in God. Hard times are blessings because they give us the opportunity to live by faith, faith that we do not live for this world but for the eternity to come.

My final prayer for you is this: 'That the God of our Lord Jesus Christ, the Father of glory, may give to you a spirit of wisdom and of revelation in the knowledge of Him. I pray that the eyes of your heart may be enlightened, so that you will know what is the hope of His calling, what are the riches of the glory of His inheritance in the saints, and what is the surpassing greatness of His power towards us who believe.'[21]

VERSE REFRENCES

1) **2 Timothy 3:12**
2) **Hebrews 11:25**
3) **Hebrews 11:26**
4) **Hebrews 11:35-38**
5) **Hebrews 11:16**
6) **2 Corinthians 11:23-28**
7) **Philippians 3:8**
8) **Philippians 3:10-11**
9) **Philippians 3:12**
10) **Philippians 1:19**
11) **Philippians 3:20-21a**
12) **2 Corinthians 4:17-18**
13) **2 Corinthians 5:9-10**
14) **I Peter 1:4**
15) **I John 3:2**
16) **Colossians 3:2**
17) **I Peter 1:4-7**
18) **Ephesians 2:10**
19) **Galatians 2:20**
20) **Romans 1:17b**
21) **Ephesians 1:17-19**

27203920R00075

Made in the USA
Charleston, SC
05 March 2014